FULL OF
Promise

KATE GAVIN

BELLA
BOOKS
2019

Bella Books, Inc.
P.O. Box 10543
Tallahassee, FL 32302

Printed in the United States of America on acid-free paper.

First Bella Books Edition 2019

Editor: Ann Roberts
Cover Designer: Judith Fellows

ISBN: 978-1-64247-039-0

About the Author

Kate Gavin is a native Midwesterner, currently living in Ohio. When not staring at a computer screen for her day job or this writing gig, she spends her time retrieving items from her thieving dog, playing video games, and crocheting gifts for family members (which they may get a year or two late).

Acknowledgments

Never in a million years did I ever think I could or would write a book. I'm sure my high school English teacher would think the same thing. Somehow, I did and I have numerous people to thank for their help along the way.

First, a huge round of thanks to everyone at Bella Books, especially my editor, Ann. This whole writing/publishing journey has been quite surreal and you all have made this experience exciting and rather painless.

Many thanks to Meg for being one of my first beta readers. I'm excited and nervous for you to see how far the story has come!

Britt, your feedback has been invaluable. Thank you so much for taking the time to help me with plotting and structure. All of those random text questions will stop. At least until the next MS.

Em, thank you for letting me pester you with so many questions and all of those messages of me freaking out about this process. But most of all, thank you for your friendship and encouragement. You're right—writing is hard.

And finally, Andy. I still question how I got so lucky to have you in my life. Throughout all of this, you had the ability to talk me down from all of my doubt and panic, and I can never say thank you enough for that. I love you. You are my heart and my home.

Dedication

This book is for all the folks who don't label themselves as lesbian or gay or straight. It's for those who are bi, pan, queer, fluid, ace, or any other label you want. Or no label at all.

You are loved.

You are amazing.

Most importantly, you are valid.

CHAPTER ONE

Rolling her book cart into the nonfiction section, Cameron Leoni nodded along to the beat of the song coming through her earbuds. Working at the library had its advantages. She spent most of her time reshelving books which meant very little interaction with other people. Plus, since starting her job at the beginning of the summer, she spent the hottest part of the year in an air-conditioned building.

Her parents had made it clear that she would need scholarships for college, and if she didn't want to take out too many loans, she would need to earn that money herself. One day, she had taken her younger brothers, Josh and Ethan, to the library and saw they were hiring. By the end of that week, she was working her first shift.

Cameron stopped at the necessary aisle and grabbed three books from her cart. She looked up and saw a familiar face. She had seen this girl in the library three times so far, not that she was counting or anything. But every time, a weird feeling formed in the pit of her stomach. She was a couple inches taller than Cam, with dark blond hair and a nice athletic body. She sported her typical pensive reflection as she browsed several titles. They hadn't said a word to each other yet, but every smile they exchanged made Cam's heart beat a little faster.

When the other girl looked up and smiled, Cam clumsily dropped the book in her right hand, causing several folks to whisper, "shhh." Heat rose in her cheeks, embarrassed that she looked like a klutz. She bent to pick up the book and held it with the others in front of her chest.

Pulling out her earbuds, she whispered, "Sorry. I didn't mean to disturb you."

"It's okay. You didn't."

Cam nodded and took a deep breath.

"Hi," the other girl whispered.

"H-hi. Can I help—" An arm lightly wrapped around her waist from behind and a kiss was placed on her cheek.

"I found you," Cam's boyfriend, Danny, said happily.

Cam watched the other girl's smile dim as she turned and walked away. Cam held back a sigh as she turned to Danny. He bent down and gave her a quick kiss.

"What are you doing here?"

"I'm finally able to pick up my last summer reading book. Figured I'd find you and say hi."

"Oh, okay. Can't believe you're on your last one already. We still have another month of break."

"Well, I'm not a procrastinator like someone I know," he replied with a wink.

She placed her hand on her chest, attempting an innocent and clueless look. "I have no idea who you're talking about. While I enjoy reading for fun, reading from a book list means the summer is almost over."

"Right." He paused as he looked her up and down. "You look great today."

Cam blushed as she looked down at her standard T-shirt and jeans combination. "Thanks. So do you." His shaggy brown hair fell just right across his forehead and he was sporting a tan from his outdoor cross-country workouts. He was tall and a little skinny, but his good looks had captivated Cam ever since they were paired up on an English project last year.

"Thanks. I was thinking we could go out to eat at Bruno's tonight. Does that sound good?"

"Sounds great."

"Awesome," he replied with a wide smile. "I'll pick you up at seven."

"I'll see you tonight." She stood on her tiptoes for another kiss and then watched as he disappeared around the corner.

Looking down the aisle again, she felt a hint of disappointment that Danny had interrupted her conversation with the girl. Something about her intrigued Cam. She wasn't sure if it was the way her eyebrows furrowed as she concentrated on her book search or the way one corner of her mouth quirked in a small smile each time she made eye contact with Cam. Those little habits stuck with Cam and made her feel slightly strange—like she wanted to get to know her or throw up, possibly all at the same time. The girl was pretty. That was obvious. But, so was her best friend, Claire, and she certainly didn't make Cam's heart beat faster.

Her physical reaction to this girl wasn't a first. She thought back to a girl she saw across a store on a trip to the mall with Claire. She even blurted out to Claire that she thought she was pretty. And when Claire looked at her with confusion, she had to backtrack and say she thought the girl's dress was pretty, making Claire even more confused since Cam hated dresses. Thankfully, Claire became distracted with shopping soon after the comment.

But that had just been a fleeting moment a couple years ago. It wasn't something she thought of regularly, not like she did with this girl. From the first time she saw her, Cam wanted to see her again and know more about her. Maybe it was just some sort of admiration. Claire frequently noticed and admired female beauty, telling Cam she wish she had some actress's eyes or legs. *Maybe that's all it is for me too.*

With a quiet sigh and a shake of her head, Cam returned her thoughts to her job. This wasn't the time or place to figure out what was going on. Right now, working seemed easier than decoding her feelings. After all, she had a date with her boyfriend later that night.

Cam and Danny had a fun dinner. He talked about how he was already a third of the way through the book he picked up earlier, while Cam tried to persuade him that waiting to read it like she did was really the best policy. For some strange reason, he didn't agree.

Danny drove them back to Cam's and when he pulled into the driveway, Cam turned to him and said, "Want to come in? My mom is supposed to be working late at the restaurant, and the boys are at sleepovers."

About a month after the announcement of her parents' divorce, Cam's mom, an eighth-grade teacher, had obtained a second job as a waitress at a restaurant about twenty minutes outside of town. It was really a bar, a somewhat sketchy dive bar, but her mom liked to call it a restaurant to make it sound better. Her mom working late, especially throughout the summer, became the norm for Cam and her brothers.

Smiling, Danny followed her into the house. They turned on the television, but as soon as they sat on the couch, Danny turned to Cam and kissed her firmly. She responded by straddling his hips. Suddenly someone cleared their throat. They broke apart with identical "oh shit" looks. Her mom stood at the entrance to the living room, looking pissed off.

Cam quickly got off Danny and stood. "Um, hi, Mom. You're home early."

Her mom crossed her arms as her eyebrows rose. "Obviously," she said in a clipped tone. "I think it's time for you to go, Danny."

Danny stood and uncomfortably mumbled, "Yes, ma'am."

"I'll, um, walk you out," Cam said as she quickly made her way to the front door with Danny following behind her.

"I thought she was supposed to be working late," Danny whispered frantically once he reached the door and opened it.

"I thought so too."

"How pissed is she going to be?" he asked, his eyes wide with obvious fear.

"I don't know. I'll talk to you later."

Both seemed too scared for even a brief kiss goodbye, so she just squeezed his hand and watched him walk to his car. She closed the door behind him, rested her forehead against it, and took a deep breath before letting it out slowly. She knew she would have to face her mom, but she was going to take her time, even if it was only a few extra seconds.

"Cameron, come in here now."

"Shit," she muttered to herself. "Sure, Mom."

She stood with her arms folded a few feet away from where her mom now sat on the couch. She refused to make eye contact and chose to stare at the floor instead, her face burning hot with embarrassment.

"Look at me, please."

She reluctantly met her mom's gaze, but her face wasn't filled with as much anger as she was expecting.

"What would have happened if I hadn't come home?"

She shrugged.

"Would you guys have had sex?"

"No, I knew you would be home eventually," she explained, cringing as soon as the words left her mouth.

Her mom sighed heavily. "Wrong answer, don't you think?"

Cam looked to the floor. "Yes," she whispered.

"You're still using protection, right?"

"Of course." Cam nodded vigorously.

"Good. You and Danny are not allowed to be alone in this house. Do you understand?"

"Yes."

"If it happens again, you'll be in big trouble."

"I got it." Cam took a deep breath. "So I'm not in trouble now?" she asked cautiously.

Her mom stared at her, as if she was still searching for her answer. "Not really. Why don't you head on up to bed? I'll see you in the morning."

"Okay, thanks Mom." She kissed her mom on the cheek. "Night."

"I love you, sweetheart. Goodnight."

She walked upstairs and closed her door as soon as she got into her room. She sat on her bed and immediately pulled out her phone to text Danny. She wasn't surprised to see she already had one from him.

How much trouble did u get in??

None really. U aren't allowed over unless she's here.

Fine by me. I thought she was going to kill us.

Me too. Talk to u later.

Love u, Cam.

U too.

She quickly changed into her pajamas and lay on her bed. She knew she was lucky to have an understanding parent. Since the divorce, her mom had treated her as more of an adult than she ever had in the past. It probably helped that Cam never got into serious trouble. As she tried to sleep, her thoughts strayed to the library girl's frown earlier and how she wished she could have turned it into a smile.

CHAPTER TWO

On the last day of July, an obnoxious alarm woke Cam out of a deep sleep. As she rolled over to shut off her phone, she ran her free hand across her face, trying to feel semi-human. First day of soccer tryouts, and since she was a senior, it would be her last chance to play on a team. Excitement, fear, and sadness were just a few of the emotions warring inside her brain.

After too many minutes of lying with her arm over her eyes, she rushed out of bed as soon as she got a text from Claire saying she was on her way. Cam changed into a T-shirt, shorts, and flip-flops before grabbing her bag of gear. Opening her bedroom door and running down the stairs, she called out, "See you later, Mom!"

"Wait! Where do you think you're going? You have things to do around the house!"

"It's the first day of soccer tryouts," she replied, trying to keep her annoyance to a minimum, understanding that her mom probably forgot all about it.

"Oh...right..."

Cam detected a hint of disappointment in her mom's voice, but it was probably just her imagination. It wasn't that her mom didn't care about what was going on in her life; She just had been working so many hours lately. Cam wasn't surprised her mom kept forgetting her schedule—she probably had trouble keeping track of her own. Cam tried to be understanding, but the added responsibilities of taking care of her brothers and doing more around the house had worn on her more than she was willing to admit. She knew it was affecting her relationship with her mom because she was starting to resent her for it, and they had become snarkier with each other over the summer.

"Come into the kitchen for a sec, Cam."

With a quick roll of her eyes Cam said, "Yes, mother? Claire's on her way."

"How long will you be gone?" she asked with her arms folded as she leaned back against the counter. "Don't forget, Josh and Ethan have to go shopping for school supplies."

"What? Aren't you taking them?"

"You know I can't. I wanted to pick up more hours at the restaurant this last week before I finish prepping for the start of school."

Knowing there was no point in arguing, Cam agreed but didn't try to hide her annoyance. "Fine. Tryouts should be done by eleven. I'll take them after Claire brings me back home. Just leave me a list and—"

She was interrupted by the doorbell. As soon as she opened the door, Claire wrapped her in a hug. Cam told her, "Let me just get my water bottle."

"Hey, Claire."

"Hi, Ms. Leoni. How are you?"

"I'm doing fine, thanks. You ready for tryouts to start?"

"Definitely! I can't believe it's our senior year!"

"Do you think there will be competition for spots this year?"

"Mom, we lost six seniors last year. If we don't get enough new people, we may barely have enough to scrape together a team and they're not gonna put a senior on JV. I think we'll be fine." *At least I hope so.*

Cam knew she was an average soccer player. At their school she could easily make the team, but getting into the games was a completely different story, which was fine because she had no desire to be a star. She would rather play a supporting role on the team than feel the additional pressure of being a top performer. It was just another cause of conflict with her mother—the former star of her state championship soccer team.

Her mom said, "Well, you better not get lazy, and make sure to give it your all these next couple days. You know you need to work hard out there. I'd like to see you start this year."

Holding her tongue, Cam said, "Well, we're going to be late. See you tonight, Mom." She held her bag in one hand and grabbed Claire's hand with the other, pulling her out of the house.

"So, another great pep talk from your ma, huh?" Claire asked as she started the car.

"Oh yeah. Gotta love 'em. By the way, I need to get home as soon as tryouts are over. I need to take my brothers shopping for school supplies," Cam explained, already sounding put out by the request.

"No problem. Maybe I'll join you. I still need to get a few things. So, how was your date with Danny last night?"

"It was fine. We just went to see that new zombie movie," she muttered.

"Well, don't sound so enthusiastic. So, did you make out the entire time? Get a little handsy?" she asked with a wink.

"Ugh, no! Why would we waste money going to the movies to make out? We could just do that at his house for free," she said. She tried to hide the discomfort she felt when Claire pestered her about anything Danny and she did or did not do on their dates. Even after all this time, Cam was still reserved when talking about sex. It didn't help that when she thought about kissing someone, it wasn't always Danny. The girl she used to see at the library had popped up in her dreams a couple times. That was new, but not completely unwelcome.

Laughing and holding up her hands in surrender, Claire said. "Okay, got it." They pulled into a parking spot next to the soccer field and grabbed their bags before making their way toward the benches on the sideline. "Wanna warm up?"

Cam tied her cleats and grabbed a ball from the team bag as other girls trickled onto the field. "Sure. Let's go." They jogged a lap in relative silence and then passed the ball back and forth at midfield. With a quick look around, Cam noticed most of the girls had shown up and were warming up as well, and Coach Hawkins was holding a clipboard and chatting with her assistant coach and the junior varsity coach.

With a few minutes left before tryouts began, they started a quick game of keep-away. As Cam made a breakaway toward the sideline, she glanced up to spot her position on the field, and saw a new girl. *The girl from the library!* Wearing green shorts and a gray T-shirt, she jogged in place before heading over to where Coach and several other girls had started to gather.

Cam abruptly stopped, and Claire easily took possession of the ball and continued sprinting toward the sideline. Cam's breath caught in her throat, her stomach muscles tightened, and her mouth went dry. She wanted to attribute the reaction to the heat of the summer morning or being winded from the warmup, but she knew differently. The source of so many confusing thoughts for the past month was standing twenty feet away. *How was this possible?*

Her thoughts were interrupted by Claire yelling as she ran back to where Cam had stopped. "Sucker! Better not be lazy like that later. You heard your mom earlier. How'd you let me take that from you?"

Cam's eyes traveled up and down the girl once more until she turned to focus on Claire and said with as much bravado as she could, "Oh bullshit, I let you do that. Come on, you know I gotta try and make you look good in front of Coach."

"Yeah, right." Claire gave her a little shove. Coach blew her whistle twice, signaling for everyone to gather around her. "Let's go."

Coach Hawkins quickly gave a rundown of tryouts and went on a rambling speech about how this year was going to be the year they made it to the championship game. Cam struggled to keep a neutral expression and not look annoyed because in the past five years, the team hadn't even made it to the playoffs.

As Coach droned on, Cam's eyes wandered around the rest of the team. It was a small group this year and everyone there was either on the JV or varsity team last year, except for several freshmen and the new girl. Her gaze switched between the new girl and Coach. At one point, the new girl looked up and gave Cam a lopsided grin and Cam knew she had been caught. She looked at the ground.

Concentrating on Coach's words was no longer possible. She rubbed the back of her neck hoping the newly acquired redness of embarrassment went away. Finally, Coach broke their huddle and tryouts started. The next two hours were tough and Cam mentally kicked herself for not working out harder during the summer. But with helping her mom with the boys and her job at the library, it had been hard to find time. At the end of tryouts, Coach called everyone together, reminded them to eat right, get some sleep, and to see the athletic trainer if they were hurt, as tomorrow morning would be yet another hard tryout.

Once dismissed, Claire stopped to chat with a few of the juniors on the team while Cam headed toward the sideline to pack up and go home. As she gathered her things, a shadow blocked out the sun. She looked up and saw the new girl. Cam slowly stood and noticed the girl had eyes that almost matched her dark green shorts. She grinned again and raised her eyebrows.

Cam realized she probably looked like a moron just standing there staring at her. She couldn't believe it was the library girl standing in front of her. The girl who had been invading her thoughts for most of the summer. She shook her head, trying to find her voice. "So I guess you're new here, huh?" Cam asked. *Obviously, Cam.* She tried not to roll her eyes at herself and rubbed the back of her neck instead.

"Yeah, my family just moved here from Illinois at the end of June. I'm Riley Baker," she said as she extended her hand with an almost shy smile.

Cam shook her hand, feeling an unusual warmth move up her arm. "I'm Cameron Leoni. I usually go by Cam." Before she could embarrass herself by holding on to Riley's hand for too long, Claire came up behind her and put an arm around Cam's shoulder.

"Hey there, I'm Claire. Welcome to Indiana. Ready to go, Cam?"

"Oh, yeah. Nice meeting you, Riley. See you around."

She smiled and said, "Hope so."

Claire and Cam headed to the parking lot. Cam snuck a quick glance back only to see Riley watching them walk off.

"Man, she's pretty. I bet all the guys will be hitting on her once school starts. Hope she's not too much competition," Claire said with mock seriousness.

"S-sure, I guess she's pretty." Cam hoped her voice didn't betray her actual thoughts. Her brain processed a constant loop of Riley's smile and the weird reaction it was stirring inside her stomach. "Let's go. I want to get this trip to the store over with." They got in the car and drove home. As Claire turned on the radio, Cam stared out the passenger window and couldn't help but picture Riley and her grin. *What is wrong with me?*

When Riley walked through the door after practice, she smelled chocolate chip cookies—her favorite. She toed off her shoes and dropped her bag just inside the door before following her nose into the kitchen. Her mom was just taking the last batch out of the oven and she placed the cookies on a cooling rack. Riley quietly snuck up behind her, reaching around to grab one of the fresh cookies.

"Hey, missy!" Her mom swatted Riley's hand away.

She passed one back and forth between her hands, until she sat down at the kitchen table and put it on a napkin.

Her mom chuckled and poured them both a small glass of milk. Taking a cookie for herself, she turned to her and asked, "How was soccer? Will you make the team?"

"I think so. There wasn't a huge turnout."

"What do you think of the coaches?"

"Coach Hawkins is definitely tough, and she didn't show any mercy for those who slacked off in training over the summer, but she seems fair."

"What about the girls on the team?"

She sipped her milk because she could already feel the heat rising up her neck and face. "They seem nice. I only talked to a few people. We'll see how the season goes."

"Nice, huh? Think any of them could become good friends?"

"I hope so." She cleared her throat. "I only introduced myself to Cam and Claire, but they seemed pretty close already, so maybe they won't feel the need to make more friends."

"Well, I doubt that, sweetie." Her mom finished her cookie. "So, Cam or Claire?"

Riley choked on the piece of cookie still in her mouth. She coughed several times, took a drink of milk, and asked in a cracked voice, "What are you talking about?"

"Oh, please. You should see your face right now. I'm your mother and I can read you like a book. That little smirk tells me you're interested in one of them—so, which is it?"

She felt her cheeks burn even more. Quietly, she replied, "Cam."

Her mom smiled as she playfully tapped Riley's hand. "And, what was it about her?"

She let out a deep breath, and said, "I don't know, Mom. I just felt drawn to her, I guess. Every once in a while I would catch her looking at me, and she would immediately look at the ground. Her eyes are so pretty and she's really, really cute. She's actually the girl I told you about seeing at the library." Riley immediately looked away from her mom, embarrassed by how much she was gushing about Cam.

"Ohh, so she's that one. Just be careful, sweetie. Don't want you to end up heartbroken."

"I know. There's probably zero chance that she's gay, especially since I saw her with that guy the one time, but it'd still be nice if we could be friends."

"Just be your charming self and everyone will want to be friends with you."

Riley stood and kissed her mom on the cheek. "Thanks. Delicious cookies as always, but I need to go shower."

"Yeah, you do. I didn't want to say anything, but damn," she said as she scrunched her nose.

Laughing, Riley playfully stuck her tongue out before heading upstairs. She thought about what her mom had said and she was right. She knew the pitfalls of falling for a straight girl. It seemed to happen to every queer girl at least once in their life.

She couldn't pinpoint an exact thing that intrigued her about Cam—it was just her. She knew the only option she had was to see how things played out for now. She should admit to herself that just being friends was the probable outcome since Cam had looked pretty cozy with the guy at the library. But, if by some miracle, it turned out Cam was gay, then Riley hoped she was Cam's type.

Luckily for Cam, the shopping trip with Josh, Ethan, and Claire was uneventful—no arguments, no whining. She could tell they were a little upset that she was the one taking them shopping instead of their mom, but Josh hid it well. He was about to start eighth grade and he was at that age where hanging out with your older sister (and your sister's best friend who he obviously had a crush on) was slightly more acceptable than being seen in public with a parent. On the other hand, Cam could tell Ethan was sad that their mom was working again and missing out on yet another chance to spend time together.

After Claire dropped them at home, Cam recruited her brothers for help with dinner, threatening them with other chores. While they set the table and dished out potato chips, she tried not to burn their burgers, a task which proved to be difficult since she couldn't stop thinking about Riley.

"Cam, when will Mom be home?" Ethan asked.

"She'll be back later tonight."

"Before I go to bed?" he asked with a glimmer of hope in his eyes.

"Probably not, bud. But how about we play some video games after dinner?" she asked, hoping that would cheer him up and offer a good distraction.

"Yeah, sure," he said unenthusiastically.

"She's never home," Josh muttered as he left the room.

"Josh, come on." She sighed. "Okay, Ethan, these are ready," she said as she placed their burgers on the table. "You can start. I'm gonna go talk to Josh."

Cam walked upstairs to his room and knocked on the door. Hearing no answer, she opened it and found him lying on his bed, listening to his iPod. She patted him on the knee and made a motion to take out his earbuds.

"What's wrong, Joshie?"

"Nothing."

"I know that's not true. Look, I know Mom works a lot, but it won't be like that forever. I hate it too, but she's trying."

"I guess. It's just annoying that she isn't the one taking us places, and she isn't here when we get home. It's bad enough that we only see Dad a couple times a month."

"Yeah, it sucks. But with school and football starting, you'll be too busy to really think about it."

"Yeah, I know...but..."

"What else is wrong?"

He hesitated and eventually continued. "You graduate this year. What's going to happen after that?" he asked as he looked down at his hands.

Hearing fear and sadness in his question just about broke her heart, but she tried not to let it show. "That's almost an entire year away. Plus, I'm sure by that time you'll be happy to get rid of me," she said lightly. "Let's not worry about that right now. If Mom continues to work this much, I'll help you talk with her about it before I leave. How about that?"

"Sure, whatever."

"Okay, now get your butt downstairs and eat dinner. Letting it get cold isn't going to improve the taste," she joked.

"Yeah, no shit."

"Watch it, young man," she replied with as much seriousness as she could while playfully pushing him out of his room.

Later that night, after she made sure the boys were in bed, she headed upstairs to her room to call Claire.

"Hey there! How was the rest of your night?" Claire asked.

"Oh, no big deal. Made Josh and Ethan dinner and then we played some video games. Turns out Josh is more upset about my mom working all the time than I thought. He seems to be freaking out about me graduating. I don't know what to do about it."

"That sucks, dude. I'm sorry. Does your mom know?"

"No, but I told him we should talk to her if she keeps working all the time. How was your night?"

"Okay. I didn't do much. Had dinner with my parents. And I just got done talking with Luke actually," she said quietly. Luke was also a senior who ran on the cross-country team with Danny, and they were pretty good friends. He and Claire had been exchanging texts after talking at a party a few weeks before.

"Oh yeah? How'd that go? You guys gonna go out sometime?"

"I hope so. I know we've all hung out before, but I think we might go to the party this weekend together. That okay? You and Danny gonna come with us?"

"Probably. We haven't really talked about it. I think we're supposed to go out Friday night. I'll talk to him about it then. So, how do you think the team will be this year?"

"I don't know. You know we usually suck so I'm just expecting that to continue. The only girl we haven't seen play is the new girl. Riley, right?"

"Um, yeah, that's it. She seemed pretty fast so maybe she'll be able to create some scoring opportunities."

"Yeah, hopefully. Jesus, it'd be nice to win more than half our games for our senior year. Ah shit, it's late and practice is going to come early. I'm going to miss my routine of waking up at ten."

"Well, it's just gonna get worse once school starts."

After saying goodbye, Cam decided to get ready for bed and not wait up for her mom to get home, because she didn't want her to ask about how the night was or the boys. She was not ready to have that conversation just yet. Avoidance seemed like an easier option for the time being.

She went through her usual nighttime routine and then lay on her bed and reached for the current book she was reading.

After glancing at her clock, she realized ten minutes had passed and she hadn't even turned a page. She thought about Josh and then surprisingly her thoughts turned to Riley and that grin of hers.

Why does she keep popping up in my brain? Her mind raced with thoughts and confusion. She thought Riley was pretty and she wouldn't be opposed to seeing that smile of hers again, but she knew she needed to stop thinking this way. Riley wouldn't be the first girl she'd had a crush on. She tried to tell herself it was more about wanting to be them than be with them, but in the back of her mind she knew it was more than that.

But now she didn't know why she couldn't ignore her feelings like she had always done before. It wasn't like she was going to do anything about it and she was not going to tell anyone. She was with Danny and everyone around them thought they were a great couple. She loved him, even though she was questioning if that really meant anything anymore.

"Ugh, I cannot think about that right now," she muttered as she shut off the light and got under the covers. But she knew sleep would probably be elusive.

After eating dinner and watching a movie with her parents, Riley went upstairs to her bedroom for a video chat with her ex-girlfriend, Abby. They had only broken up a couple months before Riley left Illinois. For the first month after the move, they sporadically communicated with each other, which consisted of a few random texts every week or so. It felt as if they had had an unspoken agreement to take a little time away from each other in hopes that it would make the breakup easier. They could individually focus on how their days would go without seeing each other all the time. The second month brought more communication through phone calls and more texts. So, when Abby texted earlier that day asking to chat, Riley said yes immediately because she truly missed seeing her friend.

Within seconds of logging on, Abby's video call alert popped up. "Well, a little antsy, aren't we?" she said with a smile.

"Come on. I know you are too. I haven't seen your face in two months!" Abby replied with a matching smile.

"Okay, okay. You got me. It's really good to see you, Abby."

"You too." They spent a moment just looking at each other before Abby spoke again. "So, tell me what's been going on? How's Indy? How are your folks? Meet any new people yet? Have you started soccer?"

"Well, hell, just bombard me with questions, why don't ya?" she asked playfully and Abby offered a not-so-innocent shrug in response. Riley summarized her day in the same rapid-fire fashion. "Phew, did I answer them all?" she asked as she pretended to wipe the sweat off her forehead with the back of her hand.

Laughing, Abby replied, "You did. You were a little short on details, though. How does the team look?"

"It's still early. And I don't think they've had the best history in terms of winning, but there seem to be some pretty good athletes on the team. Only time will tell, but it should be interesting. I'm just excited to play again. I've been going a little stir-crazy sitting inside most of the summer."

"But, I'm sure you've been getting your runs in. You could never give those up."

"You're right."

Riley was never able to sit still for too long, especially if she didn't get a run in for the day. Running and soccer were outlets for stress, but running also helped her organize her thoughts. If something was weighing heavily on her mind or if she had a big test coming up, she would go out for a run. Most of the time she came home with a clear head and a precise plan for tackling whatever problems she faced. It was rare for her to come home with her brain more jumbled than when she left.

"So, what are the girls like? Are they nice?"

She couldn't stop the heat rising to her cheeks. "Yeah, they seem pretty nice so far. I only introduced myself to a couple people."

"Riley Baker! Are you blushing? Who is she?"

Her hands immediately went to her face. "I am not!"

"Oh, you totally are!"

"It's no one, Abby. She's probably straight, but she seemed nice. Maybe she'll be a friend."

"Mmm. What's her name?"

"Cameron, oh, Cam."

"Is she pretty?"

She bit her lower lip and said, "Yeah, she is. She's a little shorter than me, has brown hair and these big brown eyes. I felt like I was going to embarrass myself every time I thought she caught me looking at her."

"Damn, you've got it bad, Riley."

"Stop, it's nothing. So, what about you? Have you met any new ladies?"

Abby let out a dramatic sigh and replied, "No. But I don't know how any could compare to you."

"Well, obviously. I am pretty great."

"I've actually been pretty busy this summer," Abby said. "I told you my uncle got me a job at his law firm. I just file papers and get coffee, but I'm really hoping to learn a lot as I get to know the attorneys and feel more comfortable asking questions. We start practice for the debate team the second week of school. So my goal is to learn some tips from some of the lawyers. I think we could win state this year."

"That's great, Abby. If anyone can do it, you can. Think you'll be captain this year?"

"I think I have a really good chance. There's only two other seniors, but they don't have as much experience as I do. We'll have a week of practice, and then those that want to be captain will have a debate. The rest of the team votes after that."

"Well, you're going to kick ass like usual. I'm sorry I won't be there to cheer you on this year."

"No worries. But I should get going, early day again. Don't swoon over Cam the entire time," Abby said before making a bunch of kissing noises.

"Shut up. I'll talk to you later."

Riley shut her laptop. She was happy Abby hadn't been weirded out when she talked about Cam. It was the first time either of them had mentioned even the possibility of someone else, and Abby just rolled with the punches and teased her about it, which was the best thing she could have done. But that teasing brought Cam to the forefront of Riley's mind.

As she brushed her teeth, she replayed officially meeting Cam. Her eyes, her shyness, the way she would rub the back of her neck with her hand. Riley knew she wanted to find out what brought about that nervous tic. Was it her? Or would it have happened with any new person Cam met? She found Cam intriguing and she was looking forward to learning more about her. As she tried to sleep, she thought of Cam because she figured her dreams would be the only place where she and Cam would be together.

CHAPTER THREE

The next morning, Claire picked Cam up for soccer. As they headed to school, Claire glanced at her and asked, "Are you okay? You look awful."

Cam realized Claire must have noticed her red, puffy eyes. "Gee thanks. You really know how to make a girl feel special. And yes, I'm fine. Just didn't sleep much last night."

"How come? Did you have a fight with Danny?"

"No, nothing like that. My brain just wouldn't shut off. No big deal."

"Ugh, I hate when that happens! You know if you need to talk I'm always here. Were you thinking about your mom? The boys? College? I know you have quite a bit going on. If—"

"Can we please stop talking about it? It was just a bad night of sleep." She curled her hands into fists. She saw the hurt in Claire's eyes as she gripped the steering wheel tighter. Sighing, Cam massaged her forehead and said, "Look, I'm sorry. You know I get cranky when I don't sleep. It's even worse than when I miss a meal."

Claire gave her a small, forced smile as she pulled into the parking lot and got out. "Sure." She slammed her door closed and headed toward the field without looking back at Cam.

As Claire crossed the parking lot, Cam berated herself for yelling at Claire. She shook her head in disgust. She felt she was lying to Claire by remaining silent about her feelings for Riley. Claire had been her best friend for all these years, a person Cam knew she could talk to about anything. *But what if I tell her that I don't think I'm in love with Danny anymore, or more importantly, that I think I might have a crush on Riley? Will she freak out?* Cam didn't know if she could handle that. In an attempt to get rid of the pressure developing in her head, she covered her face with her hands and repeatedly rubbed her fingers over her eyebrows. Letting out a heavy sigh, she got out of the car and walked toward the bench.

About halfway through tryouts, Riley was on the sideline getting water with a couple other girls while the rest of the team ran through drills. As she was about to toss her water bottle by her bag, Cam walked to the sideline, grabbed her water, and listlessly sat down on the end of the bench. Cam took a drink, placed her elbows on her knees, and rested her head in her free hand. Riley had learned Coach Hawkins hated it when the girls socialized during breaks. A few girls had already gotten in trouble for doing it earlier in the practice, but Riley sensed something was wrong, and she refused to ignore it, even if it saved her from getting yelled at by Coach. She wondered if Cam's mood had anything to do with Claire, because she noticed they had been clearly avoiding each other since stepping onto the field.

Riley made sure to take her water with her as she walked over to sit next to Cam, hoping it would signal to Coach that she still needed a rest.

"Hey."

Cam sat up and met her gaze. "Oh, hey, Riley," Cam said, injecting a bit of cheer into her voice which was obviously forced.

Riley immediately saw the uneasiness in her eyes. "Everything okay?"

"What? Yeah, I'm fine," she replied quickly as she sat up a little straighter.

Riley could tell she wasn't fine, but she didn't want to push her since she didn't know her well. Instead of pressing Cam on her obvious discomfort, she decided to change subjects. "You were looking good out there. You've got a nice touch."

"Thanks. I've noticed you're pretty fast. It'll be hard for other teams to keep up with you."

As Riley noticed the slight blush covering Cam's cheeks, she gave her a small smile, and said, "Thanks."

Just as she was about to ask Cam if she wanted to hang out sometime, Coach Hawkins yelled from midfield, "Baker! Leoni! Get off your butts! This isn't social hour!"

They quickly stood and threw their water bottles to the side. Riley playfully bumped her shoulder against Cam's and whispered as they jogged back out to join the team, "Whoops, sorry about that. I didn't mean to get you in trouble."

"Don't worry about it."

At the end of tryouts, Riley quickly changed her shoes, put her stuff in her bag, and walked over to Cam. "Hey, Cam, I was—"

But, she was interrupted when Claire walked past and muttered a brusque, "Let's go." She didn't acknowledge Riley or even wait to see if Cam followed as she continued toward the parking lot.

Cam sighed and finished changing out of her cleats. She threw them in her bag and slung it over her shoulder. Offering Riley a small smile, she said, "See you tomorrow."

"Yeah, sure. See ya, Cam," she muttered as she gave a half-hearted wave that Cam didn't even notice. *Well, that didn't go as smoothly as I wanted.* Riley shook her head, grabbing her bag to head to the parking lot as well.

Before Cam even got into the car, she knew Claire was pissed. Normally, they would chat or joke around during and after practice, but the only words Claire had uttered were the ones she said as she stormed past her on the way to the car. Cam hated confrontation and did everything possible to avoid it. She knew she had been harsh in the car earlier and should apologize for it, but she was having a hard time forming the words as Claire drove her home.

Too soon, the car ride was over and Claire had parked in Cam's driveway. Cam had constantly rubbed her sweaty palms on her shorts since the drive began. She took a deep breath and quietly said, "I'm sorry, Claire. I didn't mean to rip your head off earlier." She hesitantly looked at her and noticed her jaw was clenched.

It was a couple seconds before Claire moved at all, resting her hands in her lap. Without looking up, she muttered, "It's fine."

"No, it's not. I can tell you're upset. It had nothing to do with you, and I shouldn't have yelled at you." Cam shrugged and stared out the window. "I guess I've just had a lot on my mind, and my brain wouldn't shut off last night, so it turned me into a grump this morning."

Claire's gaze softened as she looked at Cam with concern. "What's wrong?"

"I don't know. Nothing really."

"Jesus! It must be something if it's keeping you up at night. You know you can talk to me about anything. Maybe I can help."

Was that true? Could she? Cam trusted Claire, but she still felt a need to hide this strange pull she felt toward Riley. She was just so confused.

Instead, she said, "I don't know. I guess I've just been stressed now that school is about to start. My mom needs my help with the boys so much lately. She'll have fewer hours at the restaurant now that she'll be teaching again, but what about me? I need to keep my grades up for scholarships. I still need to work at the library, and now soccer will take up a lot of my time. I guess I'm just feeling a little overwhelmed."

Claire reached over and gently gripped her forearm. "I didn't know that. I guess I always assumed you had everything under control. Why haven't you said anything before this?"

Cam shrugged and said, "My parents are expecting me to just go with the flow with all this added responsibility. I know they look to me as the oldest to be a good example for Josh and Ethan. I don't want to let them down, and I thought I was handling it just fine. Guess that's not the case."

"I'm sorry, Cam. If you ever need help with the boys or schoolwork, you know I'm here for you. I always will be."

With that, Cam looked up at Claire and squeezed her hand. "Thanks, Claire. I appreciate that. I'll talk to you later."

"See ya," Claire replied as she gave Cam's arm one final squeeze.

As soon as Cam was in the house, she leaned back against the front door and closed her eyes. She was feeling like shit for not telling Claire the truth, but how could she verbalize it when she wasn't sure what was going on herself?

* * *

After one more day of tryouts, Cam, Claire, and Riley officially made the varsity team. Then for two weeks, Coach Hawkins worked them as hard as possible to get ready for the start of the season. When Cam wasn't at soccer or working at the library, she found time to hang out with Claire and Danny, knowing that once school started on Monday, she would have even less time for her friend and boyfriend.

At the end of practice that Friday, Claire and Cam grabbed their stuff. Cam finished exchanging her cleats for flip-flops and threw her bag over her shoulder. "So, Danny and I are going to the movies tonight. Want to come?"

Laughing, Claire said, "No, I'm not hijacking your date. You guys are definitely going to the party tomorrow night, though, right?"

As Cam was about to answer, Riley joined them and said, "What party?"

"Oh, one of the football players always throws a huge beginning of the year party. I'm meeting Cam and Danny there. You should try to come by, Riley."

"Yeah, that'd be great! I still haven't met anyone else besides the girls on the team. Can you text me the address, Cam? Here, put your number in my phone." Riley gave Cam her phone and Cam dutifully put in her name and number before handing it back. "Thanks. I just called yours, so you have my number. I'll see you guys tomorrow."

Cam watched Riley as she headed toward the parking lot. She finally got back to packing her gear once Claire snapped her fingers in front of Cam's face and said, "Earth to Cam. You okay?"

"Yeah, I'm fine, just spaced out. Let's go."

She tried to hide a silly grin when she thought about the simple excitement of having Riley's number. Dread came over her as soon as she realized that she was more excited to get a text from Riley than she was to go out with Danny tonight. *This could be a problem.*

Cam and Claire grabbed a quick lunch, and then Claire dropped Cam off at home. As Cam walked inside, she heard the boys playing video games in the living room. "You guys better get all your playing in now before school starts on Monday!"

She went upstairs to shower and nap before meeting up with Danny and came downstairs a while later just as her mom and the boys sat down to dinner.

"What are your plans with Danny tonight?" her mom asked.

"I think we're going to the movies, and then we might grab a bite to eat after. Don't worry. I won't be home too late."

"Sounds good. Where is he thinking about going to college next year?"

"We haven't talked about it much, Mom. That's still far off."

"Not really. You know you need to start thinking about applications and looking for scholarships. Make sure you keep your grades up. No school is going to let someone in who slacks off in their senior year."

"Okay, I know! My grades were fine last year, and they'll be fine again this year." A knock on the door saved her. "Look, Danny is here. I'll see you guys later."

With an irritated look, her mom added, "We can talk more about this later."

Cam muttered, "Can't wait."

She opened the door and saw Danny smiling, dressed in dark jeans and a white button-down shirt with the sleeves rolled up. "Hey, babe," he said as he leaned in for a kiss.

"Oh, hey, are we doing something different? Why are you dressed so nice?" She looked down at her faded jeans, black, V-neck T-shirt, and old Converses.

Laughing, he replied, "No, still just the movie and maybe some food. I wanted to look nice for you tonight."

"Um, okay. Thanks. Let's go."

As soon as they were inside his car, he was kissing her again. She was caught a little off-guard and she let out a small yelp, but she went with it. It wasn't that she didn't like kissing Danny, but it just didn't feel the same anymore.

Lately, she felt like she was going through the motions in terms of being his girlfriend. Danny was one of her best friends and she didn't want to hurt him, but she kept thinking back to how she didn't mind being away from him and not seeing him as much over the summer. The idea of breaking up with him had started becoming more appealing as time went on. As soon as she realized she was thinking about ending things with Danny while currently kissing him, she pulled away and said, "We should get going or we'll be late for the movie."

He gave her a smile and said, "Yes, ma'am."

As they were driving along, Cam's phone alerted her to a new text message.

Hey it's Riley. Got the address for the party? :)

Hey there! It's 4002 Tyler St.

Great, thanks! What time u getting there?

Not sure yet. I'll talk to Danny and Claire and let ya know.

Awesome! So who's Danny?

My bf.

Ooo la la! Can't wait to meet him! Let me know about the time.

Will do.

Several times during the movie, Danny tried to caress Cam's thigh higher and higher, but she nonchalantly stopped him each time and held his hand. So she wasn't surprised that as he started to drive away from the restaurant after dinner, he asked if she wanted to come over.

"My parents aren't home. They're helping my brother move into his dorm. We'd have the place to ourselves all night," he said as he wiggled his eyebrows.

Cam saw the hope and excitement in his eyes and she knew she should feel the same, but she didn't. She just wasn't in the mood. Something that had been happening a lot lately. "I don't think so, Danny. I'm just so tired from soccer. Can you just take me home so I can go to sleep?"

Cam watched his smile fade. "Yeah, sure," he muttered. "Are you sure that's all it is?"

She stared out her window for a beat before turning back to him. "Yeah, I'm sure."

He studied her longer than he should have as he was still driving and she tried not to let anything show on her face, but she couldn't tell if he believed her or not. He nodded once and said, "Okay," before shifting his focus to the road. Once he pulled into the driveway, he gave her a brief kiss and told her goodnight, disappointment clearly spread across his face.

She walked inside quietly, knowing her mom and brothers were probably asleep. She got ready for bed, but before she could turn off her light, she remembered she needed to text Riley and tell her about the time for the party.

Hey! Hope I'm not waking u, but we'll get to the party around 9.

Nope, I was still up. Thanks! See you tomorrow Cam ;)

As she lay on her bed with her hands behind her head, she mused that even her short conversations with Riley, someone she barely knew, had her feeling more excited than her night with Danny. She drifted off to sleep thinking the party might be fun after all.

CHAPTER FOUR

Riley was standing inside her small, walk-in closet with her hands on her hips as she surveyed the clothes. Normally, she'd have no problem choosing an outfit for a party, but this wasn't going to be just any party. It would be her first introduction to other kids at her new school. But, most importantly, Cam was going to be there too. Her anxiety rose as she remained indecisive about her outfit. She was pulled from her fashion musings when she heard her mom knock.

"Riley, you in here?"

She walked out of the closet and threw up her hands in exasperation. "I have no idea what to wear."

With a furrowed brow, her mom asked, "Wear to what?"

"One of the football players is having a party to celebrate the end of summer. Claire and Cam told me about it."

"I see. Are his parents going to be home?"

"Um, I don't know. It's not something I asked."

"Don't you think you should have?"

She looked down and answered, "I guess." Looking up with pleading eyes, she asked, "I can still go, though, right?"

Her mother let out a long sigh and looked her in the eye. "Yes, you can still go. I don't like not knowing the kid or whether his parents are home or not. You will not drink and drive, got it?"

"Come on, Mom. You know I don't really drink," she replied with an eye roll.

"I know, but I still need to say it. If you need a ride home, I'll be at work so call your father. Understood?"

"Yes, ma'am." Her mom's gaze softened, and she flashed a charming smile. "You'll help me figure out what to wear, right?"

Her mom answered with her own eye roll and looked in Riley's closet. "Yes, ma'am," she replied mockingly. "Just have a seat on the bed and let me work my magic."

Within two minutes, her mom had thrown an outfit onto Riley's bed. She looked astonished and said, "I don't know how you did that. I've been staring at those clothes for over half an hour."

"I'm just awesome," her mom said with a wink. "Plus, while I want you to look good, I don't have to freak out about what a certain someone might think about how you look."

Her cheeks took on a reddish tint as she looked at her hand, and mumbled, "I don't know what you mean."

"Uh-huh, sure you don't. Have fun hanging out with Cam. Make sure to branch out and meet other kids."

"I will."

"And, call if you need to. You won't get in trouble for it. Be home by midnight."

"Will do. Thanks, Mom."

"You're welcome, sweetie. Have a good night and I'll see you in the morning."

"Have a good night at work," Riley said as she stood to give her mom a hug.

"I just hope no one throws up on me tonight."

Riley's nose scrunched up in disgust as she backed away from her mother. "Eww."

Her mom chuckled as she left. Riley stared at the clothes her mom had placed on her bed. She took a deep breath to calm her nerves before getting dressed.

By the time Cam finished getting ready for the party, she also had served her brothers a somewhat proper dinner and they were already engrossed in a movie. She took one last look in the mirror, hoping that her white shorts, turquoise sleeveless button-down and sandals made her look cute. Before she could second-guess her outfit, Josh called up the stairs to tell her Danny was at the door.

"Hey, you look great!" he said as he gave her a kiss.

"Thanks." Cam turned to her brothers. Standing with her hands on her hips, she said in her best mom-like voice, "Okay, guys, Mom will be home in about an hour. Behave! I'll see you tomorrow." All she heard were barely audible mutters of agreement.

Cam and Danny made their way to the party. As they pulled into Tommy's neighborhood, she counted about a dozen cars lining his street. Lucky for him, he lived in a rather secluded area, which meant his neighbors shouldn't be bothered by the party. Inside, they headed straight for the kitchen to get a couple beers. Almost everyone was split between the kitchen or the living room, where the furniture had been moved to the side to create a makeshift dance floor in the middle. As they got their drinks, Claire walked over with Luke.

Claire wrapped Cam in a tight hug and yelled, "Let's dance!"

Cam tried to protest but Claire either didn't hear her or just flat-out ignored her. While she didn't mind dancing in the privacy of her own room, dancing in front of what felt like almost half their class (even though it was maybe thirty kids) was a rather daunting thought. Usually at these parties, she hung back or refrained from dancing until either she had too many drinks or the rest of the partygoers had.

They started dancing in a group with a few other girls from the team. Eventually Danny and Luke joined them to refresh their drinks and dance, and they broke off into couples. Danny's hands gripped Cam's hips as they swayed to the beat while Luke and Claire started making out and went down the hallway toward one of the bedrooms. As Danny leaned down to kiss Cam's neck, the front door opened and Riley entered.

"I'll be right back," she told Danny as she pulled his hands away from her hips.

Riley looked cute in dark skinny jeans, white tank top, and red flats. She was talking to another girl from the team, so Cam tapped her on the shoulder. "Hey, Riley."

"Oh, hey, Cam!" Riley turned toward her with a wide smile. "How's the party so far?"

"It's okay. I'm glad you could make it. Do you want a drink?"

"Sure. Lead the way."

Cam showed Riley to the kitchen as Danny came up behind her and wrapped his arms around her waist. "Aren't you going to introduce us, Cam?"

"Right… Riley, this is my boyfriend, Danny. Danny, this is Riley. She was the one I was texting about last night."

He nodded and said, "Nice to meet you. I'm gonna go use the bathroom. Be back in a minute." He kissed Cam on the cheek and disappeared down the hallway.

"He's cute," Riley said.

Cam briefly looked down the hall where he had gone. "Um, yeah, he is."

"How long have you guys been together?"

"About eight, maybe nine months?"

"Long time."

Cam nodded as she took a sip of her beer. They made small talk about Riley's move to town.

"You look great, by the way," Riley said.

Heat rose to Cam's cheeks. "Thanks." She cleared her throat, and asked, "Ready for school to start on Monday?"

"I am. It'll be nice to meet some more people and get senior year started. What is…"

Before Riley could finish her question, Danny had returned and wrapped his arm around Cam's waist. "Can I steal you away for a sec, Cam?"

"Um, sure."

He grabbed her hand and guided her down the hallway. Cam turned and mouthed, "sorry" to Riley, who waved in response.

Danny took her into the room at the end of the hall. Before she had a chance to look around, he had closed the door and pressed her up against it, locking it as he leaned down for a demanding kiss. She let out a surprised whimper, which he apparently interpreted as encouragement to move her farther into the room.

Her legs hit the foot of a bed and she fell back onto it. *Okay, so we're obviously in a bedroom.* Without breaking the kiss, he maneuvered them onto the bed. He covered her body with his, bracing himself with his hands on either side of her head as she instinctively wrapped her hands around his neck which pulled him into her more firmly.

She enjoyed feeling the warmth of his skin beneath her fingers, but soon she knew things weren't right. She used to become lost in his kisses and wanted more, but those feelings were gone. All she noticed now was the beer on his breath and how heavy his body felt on top of hers. It became blatantly obvious that she was not in the moment as he unbuttoned her shorts and slid his hand into her underwear.

She grabbed his hand, turned her head to break the kiss, and breathlessly said, "Wait."

He ignored her and trailed kisses down her neck.

In a more forceful tone, she said, "Danny, wait!"

He pulled back and rested his weight on his hands. "What? Wait?"

"Yes, I said wait. We should stop."

"Why?"

"I just don't feel like it, and we're at a fucking party."

"This isn't the first time we've messed around at a party."

"That was one time. This isn't happening now."

"Come on. We've hardly seen each other all summer and we haven't had sex in months!"

"Just get off me," she said as she pushed his shoulders. He rolled off and sat at the foot of the bed while she stood and zipped up her shorts and straightened her shirt.

"Look, I'm sorry. What's been up with you?"

"Nothing. I'm just not in the mood."

"That's it? That's all you're gonna say?" he asked, his voice getting louder with each question.

She crossed her arms and stared at him. "I don't know what you want me to say."

He stood and faced her. "How about explaining to me why we never see each other anymore? Why you won't really talk to me about anything? Or touch me? Just fucking say something!"

"We're done!"

He stepped back as if she had slapped him. "What?" he whispered.

She covered her face with her hands, immediately regretting her harsh and abrupt words. "I didn't mean for it to come out like that, but I don't want this anymore."

He took a step forward and gently reached for her hand. "You don't mean that. It's just a fight. We'll cool off and be fine. You can't do this."

Softly, she replied, "It's over, Danny. I'm sorry."

He let out a humorless chuckle. "You're sorry? Wow. Thanks." He shook his head and then glared at her as he straightened his shoulders and dropped her hand. "I can't believe you." He stormed out of the room, slamming the door behind him.

She took her first full breath since she had entered the room. She turned on the lamp next to the bed and looked around. It was decorated in blue and gray and had a bookshelf full of trophies and pictures, which meant it was either Tommy's room or his older brother's.

She walked over to the door, gripping the handle tightly. She didn't want to go out there and run the risk of seeing Danny again. So instead, she locked the door. She slid down to the floor with her knees bent and her head in her hands.

She never planned this. The breakup surprised her too. Okay, maybe not the breakup with the way she had been feeling lately, but the timing of it was unexpected. She never wanted to hurt Danny, but she knew that she had. She saw the pain in his eyes, maybe even a glimmer of tears, but it was too dark to tell.

He had been one of her best friends since they started dating, and he had given her so much support during her parents' divorce. Yet, that wasn't enough. Somewhere along the way, she fell out of love with him. She couldn't even pinpoint the moment it happened, which confused her even more. She just couldn't pretend anymore that everything was perfect between them. Danny didn't deserve that, and it wasn't fair to her either.

She was dreading going back out to the party, but she knew she had to do it sooner or later. As she wiped the tears from her cheeks, she heard a knock at the door.

"Cam? It's Riley. Can I come in?"

She stood, making sure to straighten her clothes again. She unlocked the door and let Riley in before closing it again.

"Are you okay? I saw Danny storm out of here and slam the door."

"I'm fine. Parties aren't really my thing and I just needed a break."

As she turned around, Riley's eyes widened. "Have you been crying?"

Self-consciously, Cam wiped her cheeks again before crossing her arms and avoiding Riley's gaze. "No, not really."

Riley moved closer. "No offense, Cam, but your eyes are all red and puffy. What's wrong?"

She cleared her throat before she spoke. "Um, I just broke up with Danny."

"What? Are you okay?"

She shrugged. "I really don't know. I think so."

"Come here. Let's sit down."

Riley took her hand and led her to the foot of the bed. "Now do you want to tell me what happened?"

"He thought we'd hook up, but I didn't want to."

"Did he try to force you?"

"No, it was nothing like that. Sure, he was drunk, but he didn't force me to do anything. He stopped when I asked."

"Good. How did that lead to a breakup? I thought you liked him."

"I do. Well, I did. I mean, it's not like he's a jerk or anything. But for the past few months, I haven't felt like being with him anymore. It's just…I felt like I was going through the motions with him, you know? It was fun initially. I fell in love, and we've been together about a year." She took a shaky breath and then whispered, "But I don't love him anymore."

"Aw, Cam, I'm sorry. Is there anything I can do?"

"Can we just sit her for a few minutes? I don't feel like going out there just yet."

"Of course."

Riley made small circles on the back of Cam's hand with her thumb. She should have felt upset about everything that had just happened, but a strange sense of calm came over her with each stroke of Riley's thumb. They sat there in comfortable silence for several minutes until she started thinking about how hurt Danny had looked before he left the room. She took a deep breath and whispered, "What if I made a mistake?"

"Do you think you did?"

"I don't know. I really hurt him."

Riley squeezed her hand. "Breakups hurt. You couldn't avoid that. Were you happy with him?"

"For a while I was. Everything was great. But somewhere that changed. I just don't know when."

"Then it sounds like you probably made the right decision."

"But I know I hurt him, Riley. And my mom loves him. And Claire thinks we're like the definition of the perfect couple."

"Those aren't reasons to stay with someone."

"I guess, but—"

"And your mom and Claire shouldn't factor into this. It's your life, not theirs. If you're happy, they'll be happy. And, I'm sorry, but it doesn't sound like he was making you happy." She waited a beat before continuing. "Was he?"

She thought about this and tears rolled down her cheek. "No," she said softly. As Riley wiped a tear away, Cam fought the urge to lean in to her touch.

"Then it sounds like you did the right thing."

She nodded. "Yeah."

"You gonna be okay?"

She wiped any remaining tears off her cheeks. "Yeah, thanks."

"What do you say we get out of here? You can find Claire and she can take you home."

"That sounds good."

They stood and made their way to the door. Before Riley opened it, Cam grabbed her wrist and said quietly, "Thanks."

Riley wrapped her in a hug and whispered, "You're welcome."

Cam's breath caught in her throat and she melted into the embrace. After enjoying the comfort of the hug for a moment, she somehow found the strength to gently extricate herself. They shyly smiled at each other before heading to the front of the house.

Cam found Claire dancing with Luke in the living room and whispered in her ear that she wanted Claire to take her home. Claire looked surprised but must have realized how upset she was because her expression softened and she immediately agreed. She gave Luke a kiss as Cam headed to the front door, keeping her eyes on the floor. She didn't know if Danny had stuck around after he left the bedroom, but she wanted to avoid any more confrontations with him.

Cam, Claire, and Riley walked out together. Riley hugged Cam and said goodnight to Claire before walking down the street to her own car. Cam spent the car ride home in silence, but she could sense Claire wasn't happy about that. Several times Claire opened her mouth to say something, only to close it again.

As she pulled into the driveway and shifted her car into park, she asked, "What's wrong, Cam?"

She looked down at her hands in her lap. "I broke up with Danny tonight."

"You what? What happened?"

"We had a fight and I told him I was done."

"Why do I feel like there's more to it than just that?"

Sighing, Cam replied, "Because there is. Do you want to spend the night? We can talk upstairs."

"Definitely. I don't want you to be alone tonight anyway."

They made their way inside, Claire's arm wrapped around Cam's waist the entire time.

Cam's mom called from the living room. "Cam? How was the party?"

Cam turned to Claire and said, "Go on up. I'll be there in a minute. You know where to find some pajamas."

As Claire made her way upstairs, Cam went to the living room. Her mom sat on the couch with her feet propped up on the coffee table, watching a late-night talk show.

"Hey, Mom. Claire's upstairs. She's gonna spend the night."

"That's no problem. How was the party?"

"It was okay," Cam replied with a shrug.

"What's wrong? You don't seem like you had a good time."

"I broke up with Danny tonight."

Her mom stood and wrapped her in a hug. "Oh, honey, are you okay?"

"Yeah, I'm fine."

"What happened?"

"Can we talk about this later? I'm tired and just want to go to bed."

"Sure. You can talk to me anytime."

"Thanks, Mom." She gave her mom another hug and a kiss on the cheek.

"Let me know if you two need anything. I love you."

"Love you too."

She went upstairs and found Claire was already changed into a pair of Cam's pajamas and sitting in bed, texting on her phone. Cam grabbed another pair and went into the bathroom to change and get ready for bed.

By the time she returned, Claire had put her phone away. Cam knew Claire was impatiently waiting for her to start her story. She didn't necessarily want to go through the whole thing again, so she took her time throwing her dirty clothes in the laundry basket and getting under the covers next to Claire. She sat back against the headboard and took a deep breath. She turned her head to the left and asked, "So, I guess you want to know what happened tonight, huh?"

Claire looked at Cam as if to say, "no shit," but instead she said, "Don't make me drag it out of you."

Cam rehashed the events of the night. She gave a few more details to Claire than she'd given to Riley, but only because Cam knew Claire would just pepper her with questions anyway. She preferred to get it all out in the open without any questions. Claire held her hand throughout the entire story, offering looks of sympathy and anger as she explained what happened.

"Aside from him acting like a Grade-A asshole, what made you break up with him tonight? I mean, don't get me wrong, he acted like a jerk and that was totally enough reason to do it, but you guys have been together a while. Don't you think you could work through it?"

"No, I don't. Lately, things have been off with us. I just felt like I was stringing him along. I wasn't happy anymore. He deserves someone who wants to be with him. That's just not me. Hasn't been for a while."

"How long is a while?" Claire asked, eyebrows lifted in surprise.

"Most of the summer, I guess."

"The summer? Why didn't you say anything?"

"I didn't know what to say. He's a great guy. Some girl will be lucky to have him. I kept thinking things would get better. That I'd snap out of whatever mood I was in when it came to him. I never did," she replied with a shrug.

"I'm sorry, Cam."

"Me too."

"Sucks, huh?"

"Yeah, it really does. Seeing the pain in his eyes..." She shook her head and continued. "I did that to him, Claire. I broke his heart."

Claire instantly gathered Cam in her arms and held her tight. Cam tried to maintain complete control of her emotions, but she couldn't stop a few tears from leaking out. "You know breaking up with him was the right thing to do, don't you?"

Cam nodded and looked away.

Claire lightly grasped Cam's chin in her hand. "It was. If you weren't into him, then you needed to let him go. Sure, it hurt him, but he'll be better off in the long run, and so will you."

She briefly nodded and said, "Yeah, you're right."

"Damn right I am. So, how about we watch a movie and forget about everything?"

"I'd like that."

Claire picked out a comedy to lighten the mood. After she popped the movie into the DVD player, she snuggled next to Cam. Instinctively, they leaned into each other and rested their heads together.

When it was over, Cam turned off the bedside lamp and turned over on her side, away from Claire. She was still upset about Danny, but she knew she had done the right thing. And she was confused about why she was drawn to Riley and how she didn't seem to have a problem talking with her. It felt like she was betraying Claire by not explaining her feelings for Riley, and it made her heart hurt even more. With that final thought, she closed her eyes. A tear dripped onto her pillow and she hoped for sleep.

CHAPTER FIVE

A few hours after Claire left the next morning, Cam was binge-watching some TV when her phone rang. She grabbed it off the nightstand and looked at the display.

"Oh, great," she muttered as she read Danny's name. "Hello."

"Hey, Cam. Um, I was wondering if we could talk?"

"Well, I figured that's why you were calling."

"Oh, right. Um, I wanted to say I'm sorry for acting like an ass last night. I know you don't like hooking up at parties and I never should have taken you into the bedroom. And I shouldn't have yelled at you. I'm really, really sorry."

"You're right, you shouldn't have. But it's fine, the night's done."

"So, do you think we can move past this? Can I take you out tonight and we can talk more?"

"Danny, that's not going to happen. I told you last night, we're done."

"But we can work through this. I know I was a dick, but I'm sorry. I want to make it up to you. I love you."

She covered her eyes with her free hand. Softly, she replied, "It's over, Danny. You're one of my best friends and I never wanted to hurt you, but this isn't working for me anymore."

She heard him suck in a sharp breath. "But, we're great together. It was just a fight. I was just frustrated that we haven't seen each other a lot or done stuff, ya know? Please. Give me another chance."

"Look, my heart isn't in it anymore and it's not fair to string you along. We can still try being friends."

"Friends? But I don't want that. I want you. As my girlfriend. Please."

"Danny, stop. It's over." She took a deep breath. "I need to go. My mom is calling for me. I'll see you at school tomorrow."

He hung up. Groaning, she lay back and threw her arm across her face. Hurting someone you cared for never felt good. She got off the bed, hoping Josh would play some video games with her. What she needed now was a little mindless distraction.

* * *

Monday morning and the first day of school came too soon. Cam hadn't had a hangover from the party, but she hadn't gotten a lot of sleep since Friday. The weekend had turned out to be more emotional than she had expected. She had to tell the breakup story, albeit a shortened version, yet again Sunday night when her mom asked her for details.

Before her brain could once again replay everything that had happened since the party, Claire honked her car horn in the driveway and she rushed out the door.

"Morning," Claire mumbled. "God, this is way too early. I can't wait until my body gets used to waking up for school again. Then I won't be this exhausted every morning."

"Yeah, tell me about it." Cam immediately took notice of a coffee cup from the local coffee shop by Claire's house. "Is that for me?" she asked with a hint of anticipation.

Claire smiled. "It is. I figured you probably didn't sleep well last night so I thought you might need it."

"Thanks, Claire." She took a sip of the sugar-laden drink. "How was your day yesterday?"

"It was fine. I spent it mostly sleeping and being lazy. Luke called me last night," she replied with a shy smile.

"Oh, yeah? I saw you guys sneak off during the party. We didn't get a chance to talk about him. Have a little fun, huh?"

"Maybe," she said with a grin. "He really seems like a cool guy. He asked me out on a date."

"That's great! When?"

"I think we might grab dinner after practice one night this week. Just something simple."

"Simple is good."

"Yeah." Claire smiled before turning to Cam with a more serious expression. "How are you? You doing okay?"

"I'm fine. Danny called yesterday and thought we could work things out, but I had to tell him that option is definitely off the table."

"Are you sure you don't want to try?"

She nodded. "I am. I'm really sorry I hurt him, but it was the right decision. I already feel better about it."

"Good. Plenty of other fish in the sea, right?"

"Maybe. If you've left me any," she said with a chuckle. Claire was always the one that liked to explore her options when it came to dating.

"Oh, come on. I'm not that bad."

She just hummed in reply.

"You ass," Claire said, smiling with a laugh, as she pulled into a parking space.

They headed into school and down the hallway painted a bland off-white color and lined with tall, maroon lockers. They had to walk past Danny's locker but by a stroke of luck, he wasn't there and Cam avoided any awkwardness before school.

"See you at lunch," Claire said before heading to class as Cam stopped at her locker to drop off her books for her afternoon classes.

She then went to Mr. Roberts's classroom for her first class, English. Before she could pick out a seat, her gaze connected with Danny's. She forgot exactly which classes they shared this semester. Quickly, she moved to a seat on the opposite side of the room. She placed a notebook and pen on her desk and looked up to see Riley standing in front of her. She smiled.

"This seat taken?" Riley asked, pointing to the one in front of Cam.

"Nope. It's all yours."

Riley also got ready for class before turning around and looking at Cam with concern. "Are you doing okay?"

She quickly glanced at Danny out of the corner of her eye. "Yeah, I'm good," she replied as Mr. Roberts tried to get everyone's attention.

She was thankful that the first day of school was always the easiest since teachers took attendance and spent the rest of period going over ground rules for the semester. But it also meant her mind wandered anywhere it wanted.

She was uncomfortable that both Danny and Riley were in the class. Occasionally, she felt Danny's gaze on her, but she tried not to check. As class continued, her mind drifted and she focused on Riley's wavy, dark blond hair which she had left loose and fell just below her shoulders. *I wonder how soft it feels. Wait, what?* She snapped back as she realized she'd reached out to touch it. She desperately glanced around the room, hoping no one else noticed her movements. *Come on Cam, snap out of it!*

Her panicked thoughts were interrupted by the bell and everyone left the classroom. The rest of the day was a bit more of the same, luckily without the daydreaming or too much interaction with Danny.

At the end of the day, she made her way to the locker room to get ready for soccer practice. Since this was the first time they could use the locker room this season, Cam made sure to grab two lockers, one for Claire and one for herself, in the back. As she was putting her backpack away, she jumped when someone pinched her side.

"Hey, how was the rest of your day?" Riley asked. She pulled her shirt over her head and started to change.

Cam's mouth went dry as her eyes traveled down Riley's well-toned body. She noticed Riley had a barely visible tattoo of a feather on her right side below her sports bra. "Whoa! You have a tattoo. What is it?"

Riley cleared her throat and said, "Um, it's something I got earlier in the summer." She seemed ill at ease and avoided eye contact. "I'll tell you about it later sometime. Come on, we're going to be late."

Riley quickly put on her shorts and T-shirt and grabbed her socks, shin guards, and cleats and headed out of the locker room.

Claire came rushing in and dropped her stuff on the ground as she undressed. "Shit! Coach is gonna make me run sprints if I'm late."

Cam, slightly dumbfounded by Riley's abrupt exit, shook her head. "Well, would it be a bad thing? I mean you are a little slow."

"Oh, shut it! Let's go!"

They finished dressing and hustled out of the locker room, dropping their stuff by just in time to hear Coach blow her whistle.

CHAPTER SIX

The last Saturday of August marked the first home game of the soccer season. Cam was excited because her dad was coming into town for it. She had to leave for the game before he arrived, but he texted to say he was only half an hour away.

Not long after her parents announced their divorce, her dad had moved a couple hours away to Cincinnati, Ohio. He was a police detective, and an old coworker had hooked him up with a job. The new job came with a promotion and her dad became the lead on a drug task force. After he moved, she saw him a couple weekends a month and a smattering of days in between when he could make it back for a special event.

By the time she arrived, most of the girls were changing into their uniforms. The energy was exciting and positive. Everyone was hoping this year would be better than previous seasons, and if practices were a good indicator, they already knew they gelled better than teams in past years. They also had won their first game of the season the week before, so they were riding on a high they hoped would continue today.

After a quick speech from Coach Hawkins, the team jogged out of the locker room toward the benches. As Cam passed the stands, she smiled broadly when she saw her dad sitting next to her mom and brothers. They all seemed to be chatting animatedly about something, and she was left with a warm feeling in her chest. She knew she had to focus so she waved to them quickly and dropped onto the bench to change into her cleats.

"You guys ready for this?" Claire asked excitedly.

"Definitely," Riley replied. "I think I'm more excited about starting this season than all my others."

Cam smiled at Riley, and said, "Me too." She looked back and forth between Claire and Riley before asking, "You two are still coming over to spend the night after the game, right?"

"Of course," they replied in unison.

Cam finished tying her cleats and stood. "Excellent. Now, let's go warm up so we can kick some ass!"

They didn't kick ass, but they didn't lose either. The game ended in a tie, and Coach Hawkins seemed pleased with the result, as did most of the team because they had played one of the better teams in their conference. After a quick huddle, all the girls changed out of their cleats and gathered their gear before meeting up with their families.

Cam's mom made her way down the bleacher stairs, laughing with Cam's father as they walked side by side. Cam tried to hide her smile as she made her way toward them. Her parents' relationship had seemed to improve as time passed. Now they rarely fought and they seemed a little chummy when they were together. She didn't have any high hopes of them getting back together, but it was a much-improved sight when compared to the months leading up to and after the divorce.

"Great game, Cam!" her dad said with a quick hug.

"Thanks, Dad. I'm glad you could make it."

"Me too. Sorry, I can't stay longer. I have to work early in the morning."

Cam shrugged and said, "It's okay. I understand."

Her mom wrapped her arm around Cam's shoulder as they walked. "You were pretty great out there. It looks like your hard work at practice seems to be paying off. And Riley, man she is speedy."

"Thanks, Mom. And she is. It's hard for everyone else to keep up with her."

"Do you need a ride home?"

"No, I'll come home with Riley and Claire since they're spending the night."

"Oh, that's right. Well, we should get going. I'll order you guys some pizza and pick it up on our way home."

"That sounds great. Thanks."

"Great game again, Cam. I'll try my best to make it to more, but it most likely will only be the weekend games," her dad said.

"I know, Dad. It's fine. Have a safe drive back home."

"Will do, sweetheart. I love you."

"Love you too."

After Cam hugged her dad, she watched as he said goodbye to her mom and brothers before getting in his car and driving away. She only tore her gaze away when she felt an arm drape across her shoulder.

"Ready to go?" Claire asked softly.

She quickly wiped the corner of her eye before any tears fell. She looked at Claire with a small smile. "Yeah, let's go."

If anyone had asked, Cam knew she couldn't explain why her dad's departure made her cry. She was used to spending time away from him. She understood the time commitment of his job, and she was grateful he made every effort to come back to town for her or her brothers' events. Normally, she handled his absence well, but there were still times like now where she was almost overcome with emotion.

After the three of them showered and put on their pajamas, they settled on Cam's bed and sat cross-legged facing each other. "So things seem pretty good with your dad even though he lives a couple hours away?" Riley asked.

"Yeah, I mean it's still tough to say bye to him, but I actually think the move was better for the family. My parents don't fight anymore, and Josh and Ethan seem to be doing well with the adjustment. He loves his job and he's really not that far away."

Riley nodded and lightly rubbed a bruise just above her ankle, which she had received during the game. "How long have they been divorced?"

"A little over a year."

"Has it been hard?"

She shrugged. "It hasn't been too bad."

"Cameron," Claire said in exasperation.

"What?"

"You make it sound like it's been a cakewalk and we know that isn't true."

"Okay, yes, it majorly sucks, but there's nothing I can do about it. I'm just happy my parents get along now. We've all gotten into a routine and it seems to be working. Why dwell on anything else?"

Claire and Riley exchanged a brief, knowing look. "Well, how are things with your mom?" Riley asked Cam. Claire let out a snort. "That bad?" Riley's eyebrows shot up and she looked back and forth between Cam and Claire.

Cam sighed heavily. "No, it's not that bad. Claire can be a bit dramatic."

Claire rolled her eyes. "Cam's mom just likes to make veiled comments every once in a while that get under Cam's skin a little bit."

"Like what?" Riley asked with a furrowed brow.

"Geez, Claire. You're making it sound like we hate each other, which isn't even close to the truth." She looked at Riley. "It's nothing. Just things about what I choose to wear, or my grades, or how I'm doing on the team."

"Have you guys ever been close?"

"We spend a lot of time together as a family, and I could probably talk to her about stuff, but that's hard to do when you're someone who doesn't talk much. I'm not much of a sharer, so we're not as close as you are with your mom."

Claire snorted louder and covered her mouth to stifle it. "Jesus, Cam, that's an understatement. How long did it take you to tell me your parents were divorced?"

Cam just shrugged.

Claire looked to Riley and said, "Three months, Riley. And, that was only because I had spent most of my free time over here last summer, and I mentioned that I never saw her dad anymore. Cam is a horrible liar, so when I asked about it, I knew something was up, and she finally confessed."

Horrible liar? I guess I can be. If someone asked Cam about something trivial or embarrassing, she couldn't hold back a smile while she tried to fib her way out of it. But she knew she had been lying to Claire all this time about the strange feelings Riley had surfaced. *Claire hasn't really figured that out, right?* She began to panic and abruptly got off the bed. "I'm going to get some snacks," she mumbled.

Riley and Claire watched Cam leave, and as Riley looked over at Claire, she realized Claire was just as surprised by Cam's hasty departure as she was. "You don't have to tell me, but what does her mom say to her?" Riley whispered.

"It's really not that bad. Just that if she gets a B, it should have been an A. She needs to put more effort into her appearance, and sometimes her shyness makes others think she's a bitch." With that last remark, Riley winced. "Stuff like that."

"Yikes. How often does that happen?"

"Not very often, but only one comment like that in her life and Cam will remember it. Unfortunately, she internalizes a lot of her feelings. She was completely right when she said she's not a sharer—she's not, at all. You have no idea how many times I've been frustrated with her because I can tell something is wrong, but she just doesn't want to say it." Claire shook her head, and continued. "Ms. Leoni is a fantastic mom, don't get me wrong. She's incredibly sweet and you always feel cared for when you're around her. She's been like that ever since I can remember, and it continued even when she was going through the divorce. I totally see her as a second mom.

"I just think the divorce is taking a bigger toll on Cam than she wants to admit. She feels like she needs to meet these expectations her parents are setting for her, and that she should pick up all this responsibility with her brothers and her job.

Frankly, I think she's starting to resent her mom for all of it."
Claire stopped talking as the stairs creaked. Quickly and quietly,
Claire covered Riley's hand with hers and said, "Please don't
tell her I told you all that. I just thought you should know not
to expect Cam to share all her feelings with you, and it's not
because she doesn't want to be friends. It's just who she is."

"I won't," Riley assured her. Claire released her hand and
they both looked toward the door as Cam walked through it.
Riley tried to mask her concern by plastering a smile on her face
and asking, "What'd you bring us?"

"Pretzels and pop," Cam replied, handing each of them a
can of pop and placing the bag of pretzels in the middle of the
bed. "You guys want to watch a movie?"

"Sure," they replied.

Cam scanned her movie collection. "How about *Mrs.
Doubtfire*?"

Claire replied in the affirmative, but Riley took in a sharp
breath.

Cam turned around, and asked, "What's wrong? I can pick
something else."

Riley shook her head, and replied, "No, no. That's fine. It's
just that it is…It was my grandma's favorite movie. I used to
watch it all the time with her."

"Was?" Claire asked as she squeezed Riley's hand.

"Yeah, she died last year."

"What was she like?" Claire inquired.

Riley looked down at the bed as a smile tugged at her lips.
"She was the best. She lived alone because my grandpa died
when I was about five. I spent the night so many times over the
years. She would always take me out for some sort of fast-food
dinner, and then we would make popcorn and watch a movie
before bed. She was funny, smart, caring, and beautiful." Riley
let out a chuckle as she looked at Cam and Claire, and said,
"And, she had this crazy obsession with owls. I mean, she was
totally obsessed. There were little figurines all over the house,
and potholders, some paintings, and tons of other stuff. It was a
bit much, but it was all a part of who she was."

"She sounds amazing," Claire said with another gentle squeeze of Riley's hand.

"Oh, she was. I miss her."

Cam put the movie into the DVD player and looked at Riley. "Then we will watch it in her memory."

Riley wiped away tears. "Sounds perfect."

Both Claire and Cam gave Riley a quick hug, and they all settled against the headboard with Riley in the middle. As the movie began, Riley gave Cam a quick smile after Cam had briefly squeezed her hand in support. She was incredibly thankful she had met these two girls and that they had welcomed her into their group. While she was still holding out hope that something could develop between her and Cam, she felt like these two would be as close to her as Abby and her other friends were back home.

Riley returned home the next morning to find her mom had already returned from work. She was reading the paper at the kitchen table, which was her usual routine after a long night shift. She always said it was a way for her to relax before trying to get a nap. Riley came up behind her and wrapped her arms tightly around her shoulders.

"Love you, Mom."

"Well, good morning. What was that for? I love you too, just so you know."

Riley shrugged as she sat down next to her. "Just because, I guess."

Her mom looked intently at her expression. "Riley, is something wrong?"

She let out a small sigh before answering. "No, I just know we're lucky to be as close as we are." Her mom's brow quirked, yet she stayed silent. "I spent the night at Cam's last night, you know."

"I do. She's cute, by the way. I saw you two chatting before the game started."

Riley blushed slightly and smiled. "She is. Anyway, it just seems like her relationship with her mom isn't as close as ours, and I kind of feel sorry for her because of that."

"Riley, not all relationships are going to be like ours. People have lots of complicated things in their lives that can cause problems or rifts."

"I know, and I know that Cam isn't always the easiest to get to know. She doesn't like to talk about her feelings, and she's much better at listening. Her mom also works a lot and expects her to help with her brothers all the time. I just know that I'm lucky."

Her mom squeezed her shoulder. "That you are, as am I. Don't fret too much on the type of relationship Cam has with her mother. Just be there for her if she decides to open up and needs a friend."

"Oh, I will."

Her mom snorted. "I'm sure."

Her blush came back with a vengeance and she looked down at her hands.

Her mom stood and gave her a quick kiss on her cheek. "I'm going to go get some sleep. I'll see you in a little while. Love you."

"Love you too, Mom."

CHAPTER SEVEN

On the last Friday of September, Claire asked Cam to meet her for dinner after school. They hadn't hung out much as the semester progressed because Cam was busy with work and family obligations and Claire had been all about Luke. So, Cam was excited to spend a couple hours with Claire. She was also looking forward to the day when soccer would be over and she would feel like she could breathe easier.

Cam walked into the restaurant and Claire waved from a table in the back corner. She sat down with a smile on her face. "Hey. I feel like it's been a while. We haven't really spent much time together outside of school and soccer."

"Yeah...about that. I—"

"Hey." Luke came from behind Cam, leaned down to kiss Claire's cheek and took the seat next to her.

Cam looked surprised before narrowing her eyes at Claire, who shifted uncomfortably.

"Cam, I'm sorry. I know you thought this would just be us, but Luke's plans with his brother fell through, so I said he could join us. That okay?"

"Um, sure," Cam said as she sat back and grabbed her menu, hoping to hide her face. *I don't really have a choice, do I?* She couldn't believe Claire. Well, actually she could. Claire had been so wrapped up in Luke from the moment they started dating.

"Thanks, Cam," Luke said.

"No problem."

They all looked over their menus and placed their orders with the waiter. Throughout dinner, Claire had done a decent job of bringing Cam into the conversation, but Cam still had the third-wheel feeling all night. The one positive aspect was that she got a good look at how Claire and Luke interacted with each other. In the past, Cam knew right away whether one of Claire's boyfriends would be around long or not, but Claire reacted with so much more excitement and interest to what Luke had to say compared to her previous boyfriends.

Cam sensed how comfortable they were together. They already had their own private jokes, and Claire often touched Luke softly on the arm or back, which was a big difference since Claire had never really come across as tender in her displays of affection with other guys.

Cam had to tamp down a surge of jealousy throughout the meal. She knew she had been like that with Danny when they started dating, but eventually that faded, and she was now left to wonder when she might have that excitement of a new relationship again.

Soon after they had finished, they went their separate ways with Claire promising Cam she would call her later. As she drove home, Cam tried not to be upset about the night, but she was. She couldn't help it. She was starting to really miss her best friend and she didn't know if Claire was even aware of how little time they were spending together. She knew she should bring it up, but she didn't want to be a downer or seem selfish. Maybe she would give it a little more time.

Cam found her mom sitting at the kitchen table and paying bills online.

"Hey, sweetheart. How was your night?"

"It was okay. Just dinner with Claire and Luke."

"What's wrong? You seem kind of down."

"I'm fine. Just tired. I think I'm gonna go to bed early."

As she passed her mom's chair, her mom squeezed her arm. "You know you can tell me anything, right? I know I've been working a lot, but I will always make time if you need to talk."

"I know, Mom. Don't worry. Long week at school, you know?"

"Okay, honey. Sweet dreams."

"You too."

Cam trudged up the stairs to her room and got ready for bed. As she pulled back the covers, her phone rang.

"Hey, Claire."

"Hey," Claire replied softly. "I'm sorry I didn't warn you that Luke was going to meet us."

"It's fine."

"Are you sure?"

"Yes, Claire," Cam said in a clipped tone—a tone that Claire didn't pick on.

"Okay, great," Claire said cheerfully. "We just got to Luke's house so we're going to go hang out. I'll talk to you tomorrow, okay?"

"Sure. Have fun."

"See ya!"

She rolled her eyes and tossed her phone onto the mattress. She picked up a book from her nightstand and started to read. After a couple pages, she knew she couldn't focus, but she also knew if she tried to fall asleep, she would just be tossing and turning. She picked up her phone again and texted Riley instead.

Still awake?

Within seconds, Riley replied. *Ha ha yeah. You do realize it's only 9 right?*

Oh, um, yep. Long day. Sorry.

Everything okay?

Yeah, just rough night.

Just as Cam was about to explain that she was upset with Claire, her phone rang, and she saw Riley's name appear on the screen. "Hey."

"What's wrong?"

"Nothing, it's okay. You didn't have to waste your time calling me."

"Cam, we're friends. Talking to you is never a waste of my time," Riley said, which brought a small smile to Cam's face. "Now tell me what's wrong."

She told Riley about dinner with Claire and Luke and how she felt a bit slighted that Claire invited him along. "I don't know, Riley. She and I just haven't hung out much lately. I don't want to be the annoying friend and ask to hang out all the time. And I don't want to take her away from her time with Luke because I can see how much she likes him. It's just weird not having her as readily available as I'm used to."

"I'm sorry. Maybe this thing with Luke is just too new right now and she's too obsessed with him to notice. Don't you think you should talk to her?"

"Probably."

Riley let out a quiet chuckle. "Easier said than done, huh?"

"Yeah. You know me so well already," Cam replied with a laugh.

"Well, I'm trying." Riley cleared her throat and said, "You know, you've been the best thing about moving here. I really didn't want to come here and start somewhere new for senior year, but... You've been the bright light through it all."

She couldn't contain her smile and she was grateful Riley couldn't see her blush. "Thanks, Riley. I'm happy you moved here too." She took a deep breath and released it slowly.

"So, how about this? Why don't we get together tomorrow night for a movie marathon and junk food? We can have our own hangout."

"That sounds great. Want to come over around seven?"

"Perfect. Well, I'll let you get some sleep."

"Sounds good. I'll see you tomorrow."

After they said their goodbyes, Cam felt more settled than she had earlier in the night. She was about to drift off to sleep, smiling, as she thought about how excited she was to see Riley tomorrow.

* * *

Saturday night found Cam and Riley sitting on Cam's bed with their typical spread of snacks placed strategically around them. Riley had just finished telling her about spending the day bowling with her dad, when Riley suggested they play a game. While Riley had seen a few glimpses into some of the more serious and difficult aspects of Cam's life, she still felt like she could know her a lot better, especially when it came to everyday life.

"So, this is how it's gonna go. You get thirty seconds to ask me as many questions as you can, and I will answer them as quickly as possible. Then I ask and you answer. Sound good?"

"Yep," Cam replied as she crossed her legs and sat up a little straighter.

Riley set the timer on her phone and pressed start. "And go!"

"Favorite holiday?"

"Christmas."

"Morning person or night owl?"

"Morning."

"Ugh, gross," Cam replied. "Cats or dogs?"

"Cats."

"Favorite season?"

"Fall."

"Cake or pie?"

"Pie, specifically my mom's butterscotch pie," Riley clarified.

"Mmm, tasty. Would you go to a movie alone?"

She shrugged. "Sure."

"What's your middle name?"

"Anne."

"Cookies or candy?"

"Ooo, tough one," she said. "Candy."

"Who do you have a crush on?"

Her eyes widened in surprise and a hint of fear. Before she could open her mouth and come up with some sort of answer, her phone chimed. "Aw, too bad. Guess you won't be getting that answer."

"You can still tell me you know," Cam said.

"Nope. That's not how the game works. Time ran out which means it's your turn in the hot seat."

Cam let out a sigh. "Fine. It's hard thinking of questions."

"Well, now you can relax because it's my turn to grill you. Ready?"

"I guess," Cam said.

Riley reset the timer on her phone. "Okay—favorite color?"

"Red, but not like bright red. Maybe more like a deep red, like maroon."

"Quicker answers, Cameron."

Cam lifted her hands up in surrender. "Okay, okay. Please continue."

"Any nicknames?"

"Just Cam. Someone tried to call me Cammy once. I had to shut that down real quick."

Laughing, Riley said, "Nice. Hmm, country you want to visit the most?"

"Italy."

"What scares you the most?"

"Spiders."

"Texting or talking?"

Cam looked at her in disbelief. "Texting, duh."

She rolled her eyes. "Right. What was I thinking? Dogs or cats?"

"Dogs."

"Favorite holiday?"

"Also Christmas."

"Something weird that you do that no one knows about?"

"When I eat cookie dough ice cream, I spit out the cookie dough pieces and eat them all at the end."

She scrunched up her nose. "Ew, that's kinda gross."

Cam looked down as her cheeks reddened. "I'm just saving the best part for last."

"Wh—" The timer went off. "Well, looks like no more gross revelations from you," Riley said with a grin.

Cam playfully pushed her shoulder. "Shut up. It's the best way to eat it. Just like how I eat the marshmallows in Lucky Charms last."

"But, do you take a bite of cereal and then spit them out?"

"No, I eat the cereal pieces around them first."

"Why can't you just do that with the ice cream?"

"Because it's not as easy!"

Now it was Riley's turn to hold her hands up in surrender. "Okay, my apologies, oh wise one."

"You're forgiven."

"I appreciate that."

She repositioned herself so she was lying on her back with her head at the foot of the bed and her hands behind her head. Cam stretched out her legs and leaned back against the headboard.

"So, returning to the question you refused to answer even though I got the question in on time. Who are you interested in? I know I've seen several guys checking you out. Got your eye on somebody?"

She avoided Cam's gaze and looked at the ceiling instead, silently praying that she wasn't blushing too badly. "Nah. I'm not much of a dater. What about you? It's been a little while since you've broken up with Danny. Thinking of dating again?"

"Um, eventually, I guess. I don't really seem to have the time for it right now."

"Fair enough."

"Are you adjusting okay since you've been here?" Cam asked as she tapped Riley on the foot to get her attention. "Was it awful to leave your friends?"

"I think I'm doing okay. The summer was a little lonely and moved slowly at times, but once soccer and school started, things got better." She paused to take a deep breath. "I mean it wasn't my favorite thing in the world. I had a few months to prepare myself for leaving them, but it still sucked. Being busy now and meeting you and Claire has helped, so thank you for that."

Cam cleared her throat. "You're welcome. Do you talk to them a lot? Will you get to see them?"

"I talk to them every once in a while. They're just as busy with school and sports and things as I am."

"What are they like?"

That question brought an immediate smile to her face. "They're great and all a bunch of goofballs. There was a group of five of us that hung out all the time: Mike, Brian, Katie, and Abby. I've known Mike the longest—since seventh grade. We both moved to Champaign that year, so we were each other's first friend. Katie and I played travel soccer together, and she started dating Brian during freshmen year. And then Abby... She, um, she was my best friend," Riley admitted hesitantly.

"Were you mad when your parents said you were moving?"

"At first, yeah. Even though it wasn't our first move, I think I gave them the silent treatment for about a week until we had a few family talks about it. My mom explained how she got this awesome job offer with someone she used to work with, and with me going off to college soon, she was scared to miss out on the opportunity. After that, I just sucked it up and moved on. I totally miss my friends and wish I could see them more often, but I try not to dwell on things like that. I can't change it. Plus, I like trying new things. It can be exciting. And of course, we wouldn't have met if I hadn't moved here so I consider that a win."

"Me too," Cam replied softly.

Riley sat up and looked at her since her voice sounded so sincere. Could she possibly feel the same way Riley did? But before she could search Cam's expression for clues, she asked Riley for stories about her friends. Any hint of want she saw on her face was just wishful thinking.

CHAPTER EIGHT

For Riley, the fall semester was flying by and she couldn't believe it was the middle of October already. While she missed her friends in Champaign like crazy, she found that she really didn't have a lot of time to dwell on it. Developing a close friendship with both Cam and Claire had helped. Plus, she got along with most of the girls on the soccer team and she was friendly, but not all that close, to several kids in her classes.

She was amazed at how well she gelled with Cam and how she wanted to spend as much time as she could with her. They began confiding in each other about seemingly inconsequential likes and dislikes but also bigger issues like how scary yet exciting it was going to be to start college.

She also noticed that her parents seemed happier after the move. Both were settling into their new jobs, and they each had made their own little social network with friends from work. She was glad they had been able to keep up their family traditions of movie and game nights. She was even more thrilled that her mom had taken her usual Sunday night shift off for her birthday. She hadn't really expected anything less from her mom, but she was still excited that they were going to get to spend the time together.

For her birthday dinner, her parents always insisted she choose any restaurant she wanted. When she was a little kid, she usually went the route of fast-food places for the toys or the play areas. This year she had chosen a local, well-known steakhouse. It was her birthday, so she was going to do it right.

As they settled into their seats, she quickly scanned the list of steak offerings and decided on the filet with a side of mashed potatoes. Her parents each ordered similarly but swapped out potatoes for veggies—a travesty in her book.

"Okay, before our food comes, I'd like to say something," her dad said as he raised his glass of beer. "First of all, thank you for letting your tastes mature. I am so grateful that this is not another birthday dinner at some kiddie restaurant."

She rolled her eyes in response. "Ha ha, Dad."

"But, most importantly, happy birthday, Riley. I can't believe you're eighteen. It seems like it was just yesterday when I was at work and got the call from your mom that you were on your way, which meant she was on her way to the hospital. I barely made it there in time because you came so quickly. You have grown into a smart, compassionate, and beautiful young lady. Your mom and I are proud of all your accomplishments. We are also amazed at how well you've adjusted to this move. We love you."

"Thanks, Dad. I love you guys too. And thanks for bringing me here."

"You're welcome, honey."

Their food arrived, leaving them to focus on eating instead of chatting. Once most of his meal was gone, her dad asked, "So, how is school going?"

"It's going really well, actually. My grades are great, and I feel like I'm really settling in now."

Her mom said, "Sorry I've missed a couple games. You getting along with your teammates?"

"It's okay. You're busy. I get it. And yeah, for the most part the team is great. There are a couple of girls that can be mean, but we just avoid hanging out with them. How's your job going, Dad?"

"It's great. I'm working on some really amazing projects that I think will bring about more advancement in alternative energy."

He went into detail about one of the projects he was heading, and Riley hung on to every word. She had always shown an interest in technology, especially in the past couple years. Her dad hadn't wanted to sway her or push her to be like him, but he still encouraged her interest in his field. Riley had been having so much fun talking and laughing with her parents, she was surprised when the waitress brought the check.

As her father signed the receipt, he said, "Let's head home so I can beat you both in rummy."

"Bring it on, Pops!"

They had decided to skip dessert at the restaurant, partially because they were so full and they needed a break from eating, but it was mostly because butterscotch pie was waiting for them at home. The rest of their night was filled with pie, presents, and card games. And, for that, she was happy as she fell asleep that night feeling full and loved.

Riley arrived early to school the next morning and was surprised to find Cam already at her locker.

"Morning, Riley!" Cam said with a smile.

"Hey, Cam. How are you?"

"I'm okay, a little tired. I was up late working on my English paper. How was your night? I tried calling but you must have been busy."

Shuffling her feet, she replied quietly, "Oh, sorry. Yeah, my parents took me out to dinner for my, um, birthday."

"Your birthday? Was it actually yesterday?" She nodded. "Why didn't you say anything?"

She shrugged and said, "I don't know. Guess I didn't want to make it a big deal or anything. It's kind of weird being the new kid and then mentioning your birthday. It makes me feel like I'm saying, 'Look at me and now come celebrate with me.' I didn't want to seem self-involved or anything."

"Riley, I wouldn't have thought that." She dropped her backpack on the floor and wrapped her arms around Riley's shoulders. Squeezing her tightly, she said, "Happy birthday, Riley."

She squeezed Cam a little tighter and quickly breathed in the scent that she had come to realize was distinctly Cam. "Thanks."

Cam looked her in the eye and sweetly, but firmly, said, "I am so taking you out to dinner on Saturday night. Your choice. Make it nice."

"You don't have to do that."

"I know I don't, but I want to. You deserve a celebration. Pick the place and I'll pick you up at six, okay?"

"That sounds great. Thanks."

"No need to thank me. I should head to class. I'll see you later," Cam said with a wink as she walked away.

Riley couldn't stop herself from watching Cam as she left. She knew she should look away and forget that the wink caused her breath to catch. With each day, it was getting harder to shut down her feelings. She noticed how Cam tucked her hair behind her ear or averted her gaze when she was embarrassed or at the receiving end of a compliment. It was these seemingly small quirks that had the biggest effect on Riley.

The first warning bell rang which made her snap out of her daze, grab her backpack, and close her locker. Now, she had another birthday dinner to look forward to.

* * *

Saturday night brought an influx of nerves for Cam and she wasn't exactly sure why. She was excited to take Riley out to dinner and had made reservations at an upscale restaurant. She decided a dress was the best outfit choice so she put on an olive-green one, dark brown ankle boots, and a long gold necklace.

As she checked herself out in the full-length mirror, she refused to dwell on why she was okay—actually somewhat excited—to wear a dress for Riley, but she fought it whenever she had to wear a dress for her mom or Danny.

She didn't have a lot of experience when it came to hair or makeup, so she decided against doing much with either and just straightened her hair and pushed it behind her ears. She took one last look in the mirror before taking a deep breath, placing Riley's present in her purse, and making her way downstairs.

Her mom looked up from the mail and did a double take when she noticed Cam. "A little fancy, aren't you?"

"I guess. Riley and I are going to a nicer restaurant for her birthday," she replied with a shrug.

"Still, I can't believe you chose to wear a dress," her mom said as she looked at her with a raised eyebrow. "Is Claire going?"

Cam bristled at the scrutiny. "It's no big deal. And no, she's probably out with Luke. I won't be late." She grabbed her keys off the table and leaned over to give her mom a kiss on the cheek.

"Love you."

"Love you too," Cam replied as she headed out the door. She settled into the driver's seat and turned on her favorite radio station. As she drove, she nervously tapped her fingers on the steering wheel. *Why am I so jumpy?*

Once she pulled into Riley's driveway and shut off the car, she took a deep breath and let it out slowly. She wasn't sure why her heart was beating faster than normal. It was dinner to celebrate a friend's birthday. *But why do I feel like I'm picking her up for a date? Did I ask Riley out, like Danny used to ask me out?* Cam shook her head at the ridiculous thought.

She rang the doorbell and within seconds Riley had opened it and they both stood there staring at each other. Riley was wearing a sleeveless, maroon dress with a thin black belt and black flats, and she was holding a black cardigan. Cam thought she looked beautiful, but she didn't think she could verbalize that without sounding like a dork, so she just went with the standard, "Hi."

"H-hi," Riley stuttered. "You look great, Cam. I really like that dress."

She felt the heat rise to her cheeks. "Thanks. So do you. Ready to go?"

"Absolutely," Riley said with a radiant smile.

They got into the car and the ride to the restaurant was relatively silent. It seemed as if they were dealing with their own thoughts instead of making conversation. As soon as they arrived, their table was ready, so they sat down and listened to their waiter explain the specials of the night.

Once he was gone, Cam raised her water glass and said, "Happy birthday, Riley."

Riley touched her glass to Cam's. "Thanks. I really appreciate you taking me out tonight."

She slightly shrugged and looked down at her menu. "No biggie."

"You've been so nice since we've met. I know I've said this before, but I'm happy we've become friends."

Cam looked up at her with a smile. "Me too." They stared at each other until Cam took a deep breath, and asked, "So, what are you having?"

"Hmm, I think I'm going to have the salmon special. What about you?"

"I was debating between that and the lamb chops."

"Well, how about you get the lamb and then we can share?"

Cam closed her menu with a snap, and said, "Sounds like a plan." The waiter arrived and took their orders, leaving them in silence until Cam spoke up. "So, what did your parents get you for your birthday?"

Immediately, Riley reddened in embarrassment. "You have to promise you won't laugh."

Cam looked surprised. "I won't laugh. I promise."

Riley let out a sigh. "I've been interested in learning about computer programming as a possible job, so they bought me a couple coding books." Cam's mouth turned up at the corners, but Riley continued before she could say anything. "I told you not to laugh. They also gave me clothes."

Cam let out a small chuckle. "I'm not laughing, Riley. I think that's great. So, that's what you want to study in college?"

Riley nodded as the waiter placed their entrees in front of them. "I think so. It's one of my options, at least. I mean, it's a great field to get into, and I've always been interested in tech. Plus, my dad is a software developer so I've been talking with him about it a lot. I don't know exactly what I'll do with it, but I can definitely see myself in the tech field in some aspect. What about you?"

They each transferred half of their meal to the other while they chatted. "Well, that's the million-dollar question, and one my mother would love the answer to. Now I feel like I should make you promise not to laugh. Turns out I really like my job at the library. I love books. Always have. I try to read a little every day. And I often find myself losing track of time and staying up super late just to finish a book. They've always been a comfort and an escape for me, I guess. While I don't see myself working in a library for the rest of my life, I can see myself doing something related to books. Publishing maybe? Editing? I don't know."

"Sounds like a good plan to me. I think it suits you."

"Thanks," Cam replied, a hint of a blush forming on her cheeks.

Taking a deep breath, she asked, "How have you been after ending things with Danny? You haven't really talked about it much."

Cam spun her water glass before taking a sip. "I'm fine. It's still awkward around him, and we haven't said a word to each other since that weekend. I'm sure I sound like a bitch when I say this, but I think I'm happier now that things are over with him."

"You're definitely not a bitch. You need to take care of yourself too. I know he was hurt, but you had to do what was best for you."

"Thanks, Riley."

"So, are things that bad with your mom? You don't really talk about her much."

Cam let out a small sigh and sat back in her chair. "Things aren't bad with her, and I meant it when I said Claire can be a little dramatic. Yes, we butt heads every now and then, and she sometimes says things that get under my skin. But, we love each other. She really is encouraging and fun to be around. I know the divorce has been a source of some of her bluntness, so I'm just going to blame it on being a stressful time for her."

"But isn't it stressful for you as well?"

"A little," Cam replied softly as she brought her hands to rest in her lap.

"Don't want to elaborate on that?"

She just shrugged.

"You can tell me anything, Cam. I'm here for you if you ever need to talk."

"I know."

"Is there some reason you don't like to talk about what's bothering you?"

"I don't know. I guess I've never been one to share my feelings. I don't like feeling vulnerable."

Riley's gaze softened, and she said gently, "No one does. But, you shouldn't bottle it all up. You can tell me anything. I will listen. I won't judge you, and if you want advice, I promise to be completely honest with you."

"Thanks. I hope you know that goes for you as well."

She looked down before answering, "I do."

The waiter cleared their plates and placed the check on the table, which Cam quickly took, despite Riley's protests. "It's your birthday, and I said it was my treat. And speaking of birthdays…" She grabbed her purse and extracted a small, square box wrapped in green and white-striped wrapping paper. "This is for you. Happy birthday, Riley."

"Thanks," Riley said as she reached across the table for her present. She gave it a little shake, which caused Cam to roll her eyes, before taking her time as she opened it. Instead of just ripping through the paper, she slid her finger underneath each instance of tape.

Cam prayed she picked out the right gift. She wanted to get her something meaningful and it took five different stores until she felt like she had. But the anticipation of knowing if she was right was killing her. "Man, can you go any slower?" she asked with impatient amusement.

Riley grinned and said, "Patience, grasshopper." As soon as she released the last piece of tape and placed the wrapping paper on the table, she held the small box in her hand and slowly opened the lid. She let out a small gasp and tears instantly filled her eyes when she saw a delicate gold chain with a small pendant of an owl standing on a branch. She held the box in one hand and placed her other hand over her heart. "You remembered?" she whispered as she met Cam's gaze.

Blushing, Cam smiled and nodded in agreement. "Do you like it?"

Riley looked down again at the necklace. "I love it. Thank you so much."

"You're welcome."

"Will you help me put it on?"

"Of course."

Cam stood and wrapped the necklace around Riley's neck before bringing the clasps together. She lightly brushed away a few stray strands of her hair at the nape of her neck.

She grasped the pendant in her fingers and moved it around on the necklace a few times until it lay against her chest. "I still can't believe you remembered. Thanks."

Cam gave her a shy smile and said, "I'm glad you like it. Now, let's say we head out of here and grab some dessert."

"I like the way you think."

After leaving the restaurant, Cam drove them to a local ice cream shop she had gone to since she was a kid. She got a scoop of cookies and cream while Riley got cherry. Riley held the treats in her lap while Cam drove down the road and parked in front of a small lake. It was still relatively nice out, so they sat on the car's hood shoulder to shoulder.

Before she was able to take a bite of her ice cream, Cam shouted, "Wait!"

Riley jumped and looked around as if something was wrong. "What? What is it?"

She held out her cup of ice cream, which Riley took, and Cam then went through her purse and produced a single candle and a lighter. She placed the candle in the middle of Riley's ice cream and lit it. "Almost forgot this. I would sing for you, but you definitely don't want that. So, make a wish."

Riley closed her eyes and took a deep breath while she thought of her wish. As she opened her eyes and met Cam's gaze, she blew out the candle.

"What'd you wish for?"

"You know I can't tell you that."

Cam shrugged with a smile. "Worth a shot. I hope you get it. Happy birthday, Riley."

"Thanks. Me too." She playfully knocked her shoulder against Cam's as they both turned to look over the water.

For several minutes, they sat in silence and enjoyed their ice cream, until Cam whispered, "It is stressful."

"What?" Riley asked.

"Since the divorce, it is stressful."

Cam sensed her emotions, long held under wraps, bubbling to the surface. The instant she felt Riley's fingertips brush against her lower back she dropped her ice cream to the ground, bolted from the hood of the car, and paced in front of it.

"Cam..."

"You know why it's stressful? Because most of my free time outside of school, work, and soccer is occupied with helping my mom by taking care of my brothers or things around the house. And I love my brothers, I really, really do. But on top of helping, I'm also worrying about how they're actually handling everything. Ethan is young, and he seemed to bounce back pretty quick once they split, but did he? I mean we had to listen to our parents argue about stupid shit for months before they finally broke up. There were nights when Ethan would crawl in bed with me because he couldn't sleep. So, I'd give him my iPod to listen to while he curled up against me.

"And Josh, sometimes he acts much older than he is, and he shouldn't have to. I know he's still angry at Mom and Dad for everything. They shouldn't have to worry about this shit," she cried, pain flashing in her eyes as she wrapped her arms around herself.

Riley enveloped her in a hug and the waterworks began. Cam unfurled her arms and held Riley tightly with a desperation she didn't know existed. She buried her face in Riley's neck, the sobs coming louder and the tears soaking her sweater. Cam enjoyed the warmth and pressure of Riley's hand rubbing up and down her back. Each sweep of her hand brought calm to Cam's spinning thoughts. Once her cries were mere whimpers, she let Riley guide her back to the hood. Even though they were sitting side by side once again, she maintained a tight grip around Riley's waist and put her head on Riley's shoulder.

"My mom has just been expecting so much of me since it happened, and I haven't wanted to let anyone down. I needed to be there for Josh and Ethan and show them things were going to be okay. The world they knew was completely falling apart and it was my job as the oldest to make them feel safe."

"You shouldn't have had all of that on your shoulders. Who did you have to tell you things would be okay?"

"No one really. Claire was great once I told her, and Danny helped distract me when I needed it. But Dad was gone and seeing him was awkward for the first few months. Mom was trying to keep things moving along. She tried to act as if everything was normal, but it wasn't at all. She was just so busy all the time. I don't think she stopped to think about things until she was alone in her room. You know, sometimes I would walk past her bedroom and I would hear her crying at night. I hated hearing that, Riley. It broke my heart."

"I'm sure it did. I'm sorry you had to go through that. Are things better now?"

Cam nodded. "A little. There are times when we all hang out and feel like a family again. I'm not naïve and think they'll get back together. I'm just happy they can at least tolerate each other." She sat up straight, using a napkin to wipe her tears and turning her head to avoid Riley's sympathetic gaze. "I'm sorry. I didn't mean to lose it like that. That is so not normal for me. This was supposed to be a night to celebrate your birthday and I ruined it."

"Cam, you didn't ruin anything. You're my friend and I want to know when you're hurting. Let me be there for you, and if you ever need help with anything, all you have to do is tell me."

"I'm not great at asking for help, but I'll try."

"Okay, good."

They both looked out at the water again as they spent time with their own thoughts and Riley finished up the last bites of her ice cream.

Cam turned to her and asked, "Are you ready—"

She stopped when she saw Riley had a drop of ice cream at the corner of her mouth. She briefly stared at her lips while licking her own. She was about to reach up and wipe away the ice cream with her thumb, but she stopped herself and grabbed a napkin instead. She pointed at Riley's mouth. "You have a little ice cream here." As she reached up to wipe it away with the napkin, she noticed Riley's eyes had gone dark. Then she blinked and the look was gone. She had never seen Riley's eyes like that before, and she wasn't sure what it meant exactly. But for some strange reason, she wanted to see it again.

Cam was shaken from her thoughts when Riley said quietly, "Thanks. Should we get going?"

"Sure."

Cam picked her ice cream cup off the ground and tossed all the trash into the garbage can a few feet away. Once they got inside the car, Cam turned the radio to the local pop station. She made her way toward Riley's house, each of them singing along softly.

When she parked in Riley's driveway, she lowered the radio volume and faced Riley. "Happy birthday."

"Thanks again—for everything."

"Everything? Even me bawling my eyes out?"

"Especially that. I know it was hard to tell me about it. Thank you for trusting me. I will be there for you whenever you need me. Okay?"

"Okay," Cam whispered.

Riley leaned over for a hug and Cam was immediately struck by the smell of strawberries. She fought the urge to bury her nose in Riley's hair. When she realized what she was thinking about, she pulled back rather abruptly. "I'll see you on Monday."

Riley stuttered, "Y-yeah, sure. Text me when you get home, so I know you got home okay."

"Will do. See ya."

"Bye, Cam."

Riley got out of the car and walked toward her house, giving Cam the chance to admire how great she looked in her dress, especially from the back. When she saw Riley had made it inside, she leaned her head back against the seat and thought about her reaction when Riley hugged her. *What the hell was that?* She couldn't help but compare it to how she felt when Claire hugged her. There really was no comparison. She always felt comforted by Claire's hugs, but she never craved them. Also, Riley's hug felt the same and maybe even better than the times when she would hug Danny during those first few months of dating. She had no context for the way she was feeling, and she didn't know if anyone could help her sort it all out. So, as she backed out of the driveway, she decided to do what she usually did—ignore it by pushing it to the back of her mind. Maybe it would go away.

Yeah, right.

Once Riley shut the front door and could hear Cam's car pull away, she closed her eyes and leaned against the door with a groan.

"Riley? Are you okay?" her mom asked as she passed the entryway.

Riley slowly pushed herself off the door with a sigh. "I know Cam's straight and she isn't into me, but I really like her, Mom," she said softly as a single tear fell down her cheek.

"Oh, sweetie. I know you do and I'm sorry. I wish I had some good advice for you, but I don't know what to say. She's your friend, right?"

"Best friend."

"Then you'll just have to settle for that. I know it'll be tough, but unfortunately things like this happen in our life. We meet someone and maybe fall in love with them, but we need to understand they'll never be ours. You'll find someone someday. You're young and you just have to be patient."

Riley hung her head. "I know. Still sucks, though."

Her mom chuckled and hugged her. "That it does."

She took a shuddering breath and held onto her mom for several moments. "Thanks, Mom." Her mom kissed the top of her head, and Riley wiped her face. "I think I'm going to head upstairs and get ready for bed."

"Okay, goodnight. Love you."

"Love you too," she replied with a kiss to her mother's cheek.

But after Riley got ready for bed she couldn't sleep. She lay back on the bed with her arms across her face. She was frustrated that she had let her feelings for Cam grow as much as they had. Even after telling herself from the beginning that a chance to be with Cam was going to be slim to none, Cam's beauty and personality had sucked her right in, leaving her to want Cam way more than she should.

She was pulled away from her melancholy thoughts when her phone vibrated. She wiped the few remaining tears from the corners of her eyes and grabbed her phone off the nightstand. She smiled when she saw a message from Cam.

I'm home!

Glad to hear it…or read it I guess ;)

:)

Thanks again for everything! Tonight was amazing!

No prob!

Well I should get some sleep…sweet dreams!

U too :)

She plugged her phone into her charger, shut off her lamp, and got underneath her covers. She lay back against her pillow and gently grasped her new owl pendant between her thumb and forefinger. She was still amazed that Cam had remembered the significance of owls to her grandma. She didn't think she had ever gotten a more thoughtful present in her life. As she rolled onto her side, her last thoughts were of Cam...in that dress.

CHAPTER NINE

After winning the first round of playoffs, Cam's team had a more difficult time in the second round. They lost by one goal after the opposing team scored with twenty seconds left. Bittersweet feelings stunned Cam as the horn sounded for the end of play. While she was happy to have one less responsibility on her plate, losing a close game always felt like a gut punch to the stomach. Since she was a senior, her soccer career was now officially over.

Coach Hawkins talked to them briefly at the end of the game, and she told them how proud she was of the team. Cam looked around and noticed a couple of her teammates had a few tears in their eyes. As they were released, the girls spent time doling out hugs and offering comforting consolations. Hoping to cheer up her friends, Cam invited Claire and Riley to spend the night, but Claire had already made plans to go out with Luke.

Cam hurried home to shower and make sure Josh and Ethan had dinner. By the time Riley arrived, they were already immersed in their video games. Cam opened the door to find Riley in pajama pants and a T-shirt under her coat, holding a bag filled with snacks. Cam looked her up and down, loving that Riley showed up comfortable and ready for a chill night.

Riley shuffled her feet and said, "Sorry, I figured since it was movies and junk food, it meant pajamas as well."

"No, that's perfect. I thought I would be going out again to get my brothers dinner."

That was a fib. Her brothers had eaten some lasagna leftover from the night before. When she had gotten home, Cam had showered and put on some jeans and her favorite long-sleeve, maroon Henley. She wanted to look good for Riley.

"Come on in. We can watch the movies in my room since my brothers are playing video games." She led Riley into the living room. "Hey guys, we'll be upstairs in my room so let me know if you need anything."

"Uh-huh, sure," was the extent of their response.

"Sorry. They get a little too into their video games sometimes. Let's head upstairs."

"Don't worry about it. Happens to the best of us," Riley said as she followed her.

"You play video games?" Cam asked in delighted surprise.

"Yep."

"Nice. I do too, but not that often. Mostly just with my brothers. Okay, let me go change. You can pick the first movie. We can sit on the floor or bed, um, whichever you prefer."

"The bed's fine," Riley said with a shy smile as she took off her shoes and put her bag on the floor.

"Okay, be right back." Cam went into the bathroom to change into her pajamas. When she returned, Riley had picked out a movie and spread the snacks out on the bed. "You're ready to go, I see. A little excited, huh?"

"Well, what girl wouldn't be? Snacks and *Bridesmaids*—is there a better combination?"

Cam chuckled. "Guess not. Let's do this!" She hopped onto the bed and scooted backward until she was sitting next to Riley against the headboard. They watched the movie with frequent bursts of laughter while snacking on various chips and candies.

Once the movie was over, Cam paused it on the credits and faced Riley. "I need to go check on my brothers, but I wanted to say something first." She took a deep breath and let it out slowly. "I just want to say thanks for how awesome you've been, especially since I broke up with Danny. You helped me through all that and then you let me talk to you about my mom. So, um, thanks."

"You're welcome. That's what friends are for, right?"

"Yeah. Let me go get my brothers in bed. I'll be right back."

Once her brothers were settled for the night, Cam heard her mom come in the door, so she walked downstairs to say hello.

"Honey, whose car is out front?"

"Oh, that's Riley's. We're watching some movies in my room."

"Okay, is she spending the night? I don't want her driving too late, and make sure she calls her parents if she does stay."

"If it gets too late, I'll make sure she stays. I'm gonna head back upstairs, Mom." As she reached the doorway, she saw Riley still sitting on her bed, but her face was pale and she absently stared down at her hands. "Riley, you okay?"

As soon as Cam was out of earshot, Riley rubbed her hands across her face and let out a quiet groan. Cam had been so strong when she opened up to her on her birthday, yet Riley was still hiding a big part of herself. It was only fair that she show the same level of vulnerability that Cam had. *But what if she hates me?*

Riley's head snapped up at Cam's question and she gave her a forced smile. "Yeah, but there's something I should tell you."

Cam closed the door, sat next to Riley, and asked, "What is it?"

Riley rubbed her palms over the tops of her legs and chewed her lower lip, struggling to form the words. No matter the circumstances, coming out was always a risk and she was terrified.

Cam reached over and covered her hand. "Come on, you can talk to me. You've been a sounding board for me for weeks; now let me be one for you."

She nodded. "Right, I know. It's just, I don't want anything to be weird between us, but I don't want to hide anything from you either. You've told me about stuff in your life and I want to do the same."

She didn't make a sound but nodded, which Riley interpreted as a sign to keep going.

"You know how I told you I would tell you about my tattoo sometime?"

"Yep."

She took a deep breath and pulled up her shirt to reveal a feather that transformed into several flying birds at the end.

"It's beautiful," Cam replied.

"Thanks," she said. She took another steadying breath. "To me, it represents freedom as well as rebirth. I got it after I came out." She cleared her throat and said, "I'm gay."

Cam sat there, eyes wide. She opened and closed her mouth several times, but no sound escaped.

Fearfully, Riley pleaded, "Cam, please say something."

"How were you able to get a tattoo? You just turned eighteen!"

Riley narrowed her eyes in confusion. "That's your first question?"

"Um, no. I mean, I-I don't think it is."

Riley watched as Cam struggled to find whatever she really wanted to say, so she pushed forward. "My mom has like ten tattoos, so I figured it'd be pretty hypocritical of her if she said I couldn't get one. After I came out to her, I told her how long I had this idea, and that it was really important to me. So, she went with me and signed the consent form. And I think it helped that she felt guilty about making me move."

"Oh."

Riley sat there, hopeful that Cam's silence wasn't because she was grossed out.

Cam shook her head and looked her in the eye. "Sorry, that's not what I meant to come out of my mouth. I just had no idea. It's not like it's a big deal. It doesn't change anything. You know that, right?"

Relief flooded Riley's face. She wrapped Cam in a strong hug and whispered, "Thanks. I hoped it wouldn't. The only people who know are my parents and my friends back home."

As they embraced, Cam felt the pounding of Riley's heart against her chest. She imagined this was super nerve-wracking for Riley. With Riley in her arms, Cam's heart began beating almost as wildly as Riley's. *What if she likes me?* That thought brought an odd, fluttery feeling in her stomach and she was barely able to stifle a hitch in her breath. She didn't feel uncomfortable or weirded out by that thought. She felt excited.

She pulled away and took Riley's hands. "Don't worry. I won't tell anyone, not even Claire."

"Thanks. I appreciate it. I mean, I don't want you to feel like you're lying to her, but I would prefer to tell her on my own."

"It's okay. This is your thing to talk about and I promise not to say anything."

Cam realized she still held Riley's hands, so she gently let them go and rested hers in her lap. They sat in silence for a beat, which could have felt uncomfortable, but she felt a little curious instead. She really wanted to ask Riley how she figured out she was gay, but since Riley was the cause of her confusing feelings and thoughts, she ignored that temptation.

"H-How'd your parents and friends take it?" Cam asked quietly, dreading the answer if it was a negative one. With the way Riley had been making her feel lately, Cam was starting to think she might need to have a similar discussion with her family and friends.

"My friends didn't care and my parents were fine with it eventually."

She was relieved but she tempered her reaction and just absently nodded. She wanted to ask more, but she didn't want to make Riley suspicious if she kept throwing questions at her. "Well, I just want you to know that I have absolutely no problem with it, and I promise I won't tell a soul."

"Thanks."

"So, how about we watch another movie?"

Riley's face transformed into a wide smile of relief.

"Good idea."

Cam got up and placed *Wonder Woman* into the DVD player. They settled back down on the bed, reclining against the pillows. Within ten minutes, Cam felt her eyelids growing heavy. She tried to fight it but she soon fell asleep.

In the middle of the night, Cam woke up to use the bathroom. When she got back to the bedroom, Riley had curled into a ball on her right side, facing Cam's side of the bed. She moved the snacks onto her desk, turned off the lights and TV, and got into bed, covering them both with the blankets. One of Riley's hands was extended toward her, and she wanted to reach out and hold it, but instead, she rested her hand a few inches above Riley's with that image in her head before falling back to sleep.

That thought came true. Cam woke up the next morning and her hand was in Riley's. Right away her mind went into panic mode and she wanted to snatch it back before Riley woke up and saw what had happened. Yet, it felt nice and natural. She was tempted to brush her thumb across the backs of Riley's fingers.

Before her brain could process the decision to move her hand, Riley cleared her throat. Cam knew Riley had noticed their entwined hands. Cam quickly pulled her hand back and held it under the covers, immediately missing the warmth of Riley's touch. "I'm sorry. We, um, fell asleep."

"It's okay. I should go. My mom wanted me to do some chores today." Riley pushed back the blankets, sat on the side of the bed, and put on her shoes.

"Okay, let me walk you to the door." They walked downstairs and were stopped by Cam's mom in the kitchen.

"Are you girls hungry? I can make some pancakes."

"No thanks, Ms. Leoni. I told my mom I'd be home early. Thanks for letting me stay over."

"Anytime, Riley."

As Riley buttoned her coat, Cam opened the door. Just when she was about to walk out, Riley gave her a hug, and said quietly, "Thanks again, Cam." She looked Cam in the eye while holding on to her shoulders. "I had a lot of fun last night."

"Me too. I'll see you at school tomorrow."

Cam shut the door behind her. She leaned back against it, staring up at the ceiling. She still couldn't believe that Riley was gay. She never would have guessed. As she remembered the position they woke up in, Cam's eyes shut and her imagination took over. Their faces had only been inches apart. It would have been so easy for her to lean forward and place a kiss on Riley's lips. She straightened up and opened her eyes.

Oh shit.

CHAPTER TEN

The Friday before Thanksgiving was the night for a big party thrown by Andre Wilson, the senior quarterback on the football team. It would probably be even bigger than the party thrown at the beginning of the school year, and everyone had been looking forward to it.

Claire drove Cam and Riley to Cam's house after school that day, so they could hang out and get ready for the party together. They all had a quick bite before heading up to Cam's room. Claire and Riley started getting ready in the attached bathroom almost immediately, while Cam waited her turn, lying on the bed channel surfing.

Riley was the first one done, and when Cam saw her, she stopped changing the channels, and openly stared at her with her lips slightly parted. She wore skinny jeans, a pale pink tank top, a light, cream-colored cardigan, and knee-high brown boots. Her makeup was very subtle—only some mascara and pink lip gloss. Riley's hair was loosely curled, and the sides were pulled up and gathered in the back by a gold clip. Cam was also thrilled to see she was wearing the owl necklace.

Riley looked down at what she was wearing. "Does this not look good?"

She shook her head and said, "You look great."

Riley blushed but before she had a chance to reply, Claire walked in and said, "Well, of course she looks great. She always does. How do I look, guys?"

Claire had dressed up, but she was known to do that. She wore a navy blue dress with three-quarter length sleeves, a thin, tan belt around the waist, and matching tan ankle boots with a slight heel. Her makeup was heavier than Riley's but not so that it was too much.

"Looking awesome, Claire," Riley replied.

Smiling, Claire said, "Thanks. All right, Cam, now it's your turn to get dressed."

Groaning, Cam crawled off the bed and stood in front of Claire.

"I think you'll look great in that red dr—"

Cam held up a hand to interrupt her. "Nope, I am not wearing a dress. I know the end of season party is a bit classier than most, but I'm not going to be uncomfortable all night." While she had been okay wearing a dress to Riley's birthday dinner, it hadn't involved dancing or drinking games, so she hadn't had much of a problem with her choice of outfit. Now, however, she was looking for comfort and practicality in tonight's choice of clothing.

Claire narrowed her eyes and said, "Okay, okay. You don't have to wear a dress, but only if you let me pick out your outfit."

Placing her hands on her hips, Cam rolled her eyes and muttered, "Fine. Have at it." She went back to lie back on her bed and threw her arm over her eyes as Claire rummaged through her closet and dresser, quietly consulting with Riley every so often. Finally, Claire picked out black skinny jeans, a white, sleeveless top, red flats, and a short, black leather jacket.

"You'll look fantastic in this!" Claire said with a smile.

Riley nodded in agreement. "Definitely."

As Cam got off the bed, she struggled not to roll her eyes and said with a hint of self-deprecation, "If you say so."

Claire gripped Cam's wrist, looked her in the eye, and said softly, "You're going to look great."

"Thanks, Claire."

As Claire and Riley checked their makeup and hair again in the mirror, Cam changed into the clothes Claire had picked out for her. Once she finished, she turned toward them and asked, "Well?"

Riley was the first to turn around, and Cam didn't miss how Riley's eyes traveled up her body with a slight hesitation before reaching her face.

"You…" Riley cleared her throat and continued, "you look beautiful."

She immediately felt the heat rush to her cheeks. She was never great at taking compliments, but she noticed that a swarm of butterflies seemed to have settled in her stomach. *Huh, that's weird.*

Claire turned and wrapped an arm around Riley's shoulders. "You do look beautiful, Cam. Told you so."

Cam stuck her hands in her back pockets and shrugged. "Yeah, yeah. Let's go." She caught Riley's gaze again briefly, but she couldn't tell what Riley was thinking. It was like the look she had in her eyes when they were eating ice cream after Riley's birthday dinner.

Claire checked her hair once more in the mirror and said, "I'm ready. Let's go."

"Bye, Mom," Cam said as she reached the bottom of the stairs.

"Wait a minute," her mom called, which made all three girls stop and turn around. "Now, remember—have fun, but be smart and safe. If you need a ride, call me. I mean it."

"Don't worry, Ms. Leoni. We'll be fine," Claire replied.

"I'm sure you will. There is to be no drinking and driving. Preferably, no drinking at all. Got it?"

"Got it," Cam said, kissing her mom on the cheek. After calling out goodbye to her brothers, they all headed for the party.

As soon as Riley walked into the front door of Andre's house, she looked around the room, surveying the setup. Straight ahead was a staircase leading up to the second floor where an unrecognizable couple made out and looked to be a second away from moving to a more private location. To the right was the living room and several small groups of people sitting around and chatting away. One group even had a game of euchre going, a staple card game in the Midwest. Finally, to the left was an open area that contained the dining room and kitchen. Andre had placed a large plastic tarp across the dining room table and the chairs had been stacked neatly in a corner. Two seniors on the volleyball team were playing a junior and senior from the boys' soccer team in what seemed to be a competitive game of beer pong, while several of their friends stood around cheering and drinking.

"Let's grab a drink. I need to get mine out of the way, so I can drive home," Claire said as she grabbed Riley's wrist and pulled her toward the kitchen with Cam following behind them. Several of their soccer teammates stood around the kitchen island talking and drinking.

Riley gratefully took the cup of beer Claire poured for her. She joined the conversation about their tough loss and how she was equally happy and sad the season was over. Riley noticed Cam was her usual self and stood a tad off to the side, quietly listening to everyone's thoughts as well as glancing around the room every so often.

Her focus was pulled toward the dining room when she heard one of the volleyball players yell, "Who's up?"

Riley quickly turned to Cam and said, "Let's play." Riley wrapped her arm around Cam's waist and guided her toward the free end of the dining room table.

Once all the cups were set up, the volleyball players, Marcy and Kayla, lined up for the first shots of the game since they had been the winners of the previous game. After eyeing up her opponents, Riley turned to Cam and said with a wink, "Time to kick some ass!"

It was a tight matchup at first—each team making at least one shot for the first few rounds, but then Marcy and Kayla started to falter, probably due to this being their third or fourth game. Cam and Riley took advantage of their increasingly sloppy shots, quickly finished them off, and cleared the table.

Riley and Cam hugged, and they refilled the cups for their next opponents, two senior football players. This game was even easier to win because Riley was pretty sure these two had helped Andre set up everything for the party, so their drinking had begun a couple hours before anyone else had arrived.

As the night wore on, both Riley and Cam felt the effects of all the beer they had to drink. The more they won, the less reserved Cam became, giving Riley hugs and caressing the small of her back. Every brush of Cam's fingers along Riley's skin sent shivers down her spine and made her heart race. It took every effort to temper the urge to wrap Cam tightly in her arms.

Their fourth game started poorly, not making a single shot in their first ten attempts. They were down by three cups when Luke walked in with Danny and another cross-country teammate, Phil. Riley watched as Danny's gaze landed on Cam. His eyes dimmed with sadness and he immediately went into the living room instead, while Luke and Phil moved toward the keg to get beers. Once they got their drinks, they stood next to the table to watch the competition.

Cam and Riley were making a comeback and were now tied, each team having two cups left. Their opponents missed both of their shots. As Cam prepared for her shot, she looked over at Riley and gave her a smile and a wink that made Riley want to melt on the spot. Cam looked toward her target, trying to hold her arm steady despite the alcohol-induced sway, and launched the ball. It went in with almost perfect precision.

"Woo!" She jumped up and down with her arms in the air in celebration. She turned to Riley, and said, "You've got this!"

Riley took a deep breath and tossed the ball to the opposite side of the table. She was probably more surprised than anyone when it hit the inner rim of the cup and dropped in. Before Riley could even process that they had won, Cam pulled her in for a bear hug and buried her face in Riley's neck. Riley felt the warmth of Cam's breath on her skin, and it took a tremendous effort to stifle a moan.

While she wanted to continue celebrating with Cam, she knew it was getting too hard to not react to Cam's touches—the beer making her slow to respond appropriately. She reached around her neck and pulled Cam's hands away. "Great game, Cam. I think I'm going to sit the next one out."

Cam's eyebrows lowered, and Riley saw disappointment flicker in her eyes. "No way. We're a great team. We've dominated all night."

With a final squeeze of Cam's hands, Riley replied, "I know, but how about you play with one of these other guys now?"

Phil immediately swooped in at Riley's suggestion. "I'm in! Let's play, Cam."

Cam took the ball Phil had been holding out as Riley left for the kitchen.

Once Riley had realized Cam was starting to become a little more touchy-feely, she knew it would be a good idea for her to remove herself from any temptation and find another group of friends. She poured herself a fresh beer and took a few small sips, leaning her elbows on the kitchen island as she watched Cam and Phil sink a couple shots in a row. He celebrated by wrapping his arm around Cam's waist and pulled her in for a side hug. She didn't want to watch another guy flirt with Cam, so she closed her eyes and took a large gulp of beer. When she opened them, she jumped back when she found someone standing next to her.

The girl reached out and gently gripped Riley's forearm, and said, "Whoa, sorry about that. I didn't mean to scare you."

Blushing in embarrassment, Riley shook her head, and replied, "It's okay. I think I was in my own little world." The girl was very cute. She seemed to be almost half a foot taller than Riley with dark brown skin, closely buzzed black hair, and eyes the color of honey. She was wearing light-washed jeans, a maroon long-sleeve T-shirt, and a navy blue vest. Riley had seen her around school before and knew she was a junior on the volleyball team, but she had never properly introduced herself. She reached out her hand, and said, "I'm Riley."

"I know." Riley's brow furrowed in confusion as the girl continued. "What I mean is that I've seen you around and I've been to a few of your soccer games. I'm good friends with your keeper, Cassie."

"Got it."

"Oh, I'm Bri, by the way," she said as she rolled her eyes as if she was embarrassed.

"It's nice to meet you."

"You too. So, how do you like Indy? You just moved here this year, right?"

"Yeah, we moved here at the beginning of the summer," Riley replied. "I like it a lot. Everyone seems pretty nice and I've made some good friends," she said as she looked over to where Cam and Phil were just starting a new game of beer pong.

Bri followed her gaze and asked, "Oh yeah. I've seen you around with Cam and Claire, right?"

"Yep," she replied. She caught Cam's gaze and noticed her eyes had narrowed to tiny slits. Riley didn't understand her reaction, but she shook it off and filed it away so she could ask Cam about it later. Instead she turned back toward Bri and asked, "So, how's your semester going so far?"

Riley found herself in easy conversation with Bri for over half an hour. They sat on a couple barstools on the other side of the island, facing each other. She learned Bri had an older brother and a younger sister. She was obsessed with volleyball, loved to read, and had a secret talent for cooking.

Riley couldn't be sure, but she felt like Bri had been flirting with her almost since the beginning of their conversation. Bri had taken every opportunity to touch her in some way, whether she brushed her fingers against Riley's or slapped her knee in reply to something funny she had said. And if Riley was honest with herself, she wasn't all that mad about it. She hadn't been the focus of another girl's attention since Abby. At times, it felt like Cam would flirt with her, but she always tried to brush it aside as just friendship. While Bri's touches weren't bringing the swarms of butterflies that Cam's always did, there were still a few of those buggers flying around her stomach.

Riley's attention was pulled away from Bri when she heard a groan from Phil. It looked like they had finally met their match and lost. Cam and Phil walked away from the table and were immediately replaced by a couple guys from the cross-country team. Riley watched as they talked with Luke and Claire briefly, before Phil squeezed Cam's shoulder with a smile and followed Luke out of the house.

Before Riley could continue chatting with Bri, Claire and Cam approached them. "Are you ready to go, Riley? I think this one has had enough," she said, pointing at Cam with her thumb. "I'm going to drop you guys off at Cam's, and then I'm going to head over to Luke's."

"Yeah, sure." She stood up from her barstool, and said, "Oh, guys, this is Bri. Bri, this is Cam and Claire."

Claire quickly stuck out her hand for Bri to shake, and said with a smile, "It's nice to meet you."

"You too."

Cam was less enthusiastic with a short nod of her head, and a mumbled, "Hey."

Riley winced at Cam's clipped response but decided to ignore it for now. Instead, she turned to Bri, and said, "Nice talking to you, Bri. See you around school."

"Do you maybe want to hang out sometime?" she asked hesitantly.

Cam let out what sounded like a displeased snort, but Riley ignored it and reached for her phone. "Sure, that sounds great. Here put your number in."

After entering her phone number, Bri handed it back to Riley. "There you go. Have a good night," she said as she lightly squeezed Riley's forearm.

"You too," she replied, enjoying the warmth from Bri's touch. She turned to Claire. "I'm ready."

They made their way through the small crowd in the dining room to the front door. When they reached Claire's car, Cam immediately climbed into the backseat and slammed the door. Riley could tell something was wrong, but she had no idea what it could be, so she just let her stew in the back.

The ride to Cam's house was relatively quiet except for the radio playing softly and Claire humming along. As soon as Claire stopped the car, Cam opened her door and muttered, "See ya, Claire."

Riley and Claire looked at each other in confusion and shrugged. "Thanks for the ride. Have fun tonight," she said with a wink.

Claire laughed. "I will. See you Monday."

"Bye."

Riley got out of the car and followed Cam into the house. She knew she would have to find out what was wrong with Cam, but she wasn't sure whether she should ask about it tonight since Cam was drunk. When she entered the house, she realized Cam hadn't waited for her, so she closed and locked the front door, took a deep breath, and walked upstairs to Cam's room.

Riley walked into the room just as Cam finished pulling her T-shirt down. She quietly closed the door, conscious that Cam's mom and brothers were asleep down the hall. She whispered, "Was something wrong tonight?"

"No," Cam replied brusquely as she stalked into the bathroom to brush her teeth.

Riley followed and leaned against the doorframe. She knew Cam was lying. She studied the way Cam forcefully brushed her teeth before speaking again. "I know something was wrong, Cameron. I think I can read you pretty well by now."

"Whatever. Maybe you need to read your new friend better."

Confused, she asked, "What are you talking about? Is this about Bri?"

"Forget about it." Cam rinsed her mouth and toothbrush before brushing past Riley into the bedroom.

"No, I'm not going to forget about it. What do you have against Bri?"

"Nothing."

"Cameron, come on."

"You do realize she was flirting with you? You know she's gay? The rumor is all over the school."

"And what does that matter? You remember I'm gay, right?" she whispered harshly.

"Yes, Riley. Just forget it," Cam replied as she plugged in her phone.

Riley couldn't understand where this attitude was coming from. Cam had said she had no problem with her being gay. *Why is she making such a big deal about Bri possibly being gay?* Riley felt her anger rise with each passing second. She turned Cam around so they could face each other. "No, I'm not going to forget it. Why do you have a problem? Is it because if people realize I'm gay, they'll think you are too just because you hang out with me?" Cam briefly shook her head. "Talk to me, damn it. If you don't want to be seen with me or be near me because I'm gay, then just tell me."

Riley watched as Cam's face went deathly pale and she ran into the bathroom. She barely made it in time to throw up in the toilet. Riley closed her eyes and released a long sigh. She went to Cam, knelt next to her, and lightly rubbed her back as she continued throwing up. Once she was done, Riley stood and filled a glass with water and grabbed a bottle of aspirin out of the cabinet.

"I don't want to lose you, Riley," Cam said in a hoarse voice.

Riley handed her a tissue while Cam flushed the toilet. "That's not going to happen. Why would you lose me?" Cam shrugged in a non-answer. Riley retrieved the glass of water and took two pills out of the bottle and handed them to Cam. "Here, take these."

Cam swallowed them with a few small sips of water. She blew her nose, wiped her eyes, and threw the tissue in the trash. She slowly stood with a groan and drank several more sips of water.

"Feeling better?"

"Yeah, thanks." Cam reached for her toothbrush to brush her teeth for the second time in five minutes, albeit a little softer and slower this time. After wiping her mouth, she placed the towel on the counter. She looked at the floor, and said, "I'm sorry, Riley. I was acting like an ass tonight."

Riley reached out and lightly squeezed Cam's hand in hers. "It's okay. I still don't really understand why you did, but let's not talk about that tonight. Okay?" Cam nodded, and Riley pulled her in for a hug.

They both sighed in relief, and Riley wrapped her arms tightly around Cam's waist. Riley was still confused about Cam's behavior throughout the night, but she understood that Cam was in no condition to explain it. She knew Cam had to be exhausted, and she indulged herself a bit by placing a light kiss on the top of Cam's head. "How about we get you to bed?"

Cam nodded against Riley's shoulder.

Riley kept her arm around Cam's waist as she helped Cam get into the bed. She gently pulled the covers up to Cam's shoulders and Cam immediately grabbed the blanket and turned onto her side, facing the middle of the bed. Riley stood there watching the rise and fall of Cam's shoulders as she drifted off to sleep.

Riley refilled the glass with water and placed it on Cam's nightstand before getting ready for bed. She lay on her side facing Cam, gently pushing a few stray hairs behind her ear. "Goodnight, Cameron," she whispered as she rested her head against the pillow.

"Mm, goodnight, babe," Cam mumbled in reply.

Riley's eyes widened in response, but she knew Cam was probably just thinking of Danny when she said it. They had only been broken up for a few months, so it wouldn't surprise Riley that Cam still dreamt about him. Riley turned onto her back and rested one arm above her head as she thought about how much she wanted Cam to say that to her and mean it. *If only.*

The next morning, Cam woke up slowly, opening her eyes to blinding light coming through the window above her desk. She was on her side facing the wall and she squeezed her eyes shut as tight as she could to combat the effect the light was having on her head. While it wasn't the worst headache she'd ever had, there was still a constant throb right above her eyebrows. She hadn't let herself drink that much since the first party she had attended her sophomore year. She was normally decent at controlling herself and watching how many drinks she had, but seeing Riley with Bri had thrown her for some reason.

She opened her eyes slowly, attempting to adjust to the light. When she could keep them open completely, she turned onto her back with a small groan.

"Are you okay?" Riley asked as she flipped over to look at Cam.

Cam turned her head to the left to meet Riley's concerned gaze. "I'm okay. Head hurts a bit."

"I can imagine," Riley replied with a hint of amusement.

Cam let out a quiet chuckle, and said, "Yeah." She averted her gaze and focused it on a loose string on her sheets. "I'm sorry about last night, Riley," she said softly.

Riley sat up and leaned back against the headboard. "Why were you acting like that? Do you have something against Bri? Do you not like her?"

Cam followed Riley's movement and sat up, pulling her knees to her chest and wrapping her arms around them. She shrugged before quietly replying, "I don't know how to explain it." She was having a hard enough time rationalizing her thoughts to herself, much less verbalizing them to Riley. She just didn't like the way she felt seeing them together—Bri touching Riley and obviously flirting.

"Does it have something to do with the fact that everyone thinks she's gay? Is it that you don't want to be associated with me if people find out that I am?" Riley asked hesitantly but with an undercurrent of anger.

Cam looked at her with wide eyes. "No," Cam exclaimed. "You know I don't have a problem with that."

"Then, what was it?"

Cam scrambled out of bed and paced the length of her bedroom. Throwing her hands up in frustration, she turned toward Riley and put her hands on her hips. "Ugh, I don't know.

But, come on, she was all over you. I mean just because I don't have a problem with her being gay, doesn't mean other people will feel the same way. She didn't seem that great. And she's so… tall," Cam said with a scrunch of her nose.

"Well, that just means she can always reach the top shelf," Riley replied as she got out of bed and walked around the bed to stand in front of Cam.

"Oh, shut up. It's not funny. You seriously aren't thinking of dating her, are you?" Cam replied in a harsh tone as she crossed her arms.

"I don't understand what your issue is with her. It's like you're jealous of her for some reason. Is it because you think she'll take me away from you or because you have a crush on me?" Riley joked.

Cam's mouth fell open, her arms dropped to her sides, and she stood stock still. "Wh-wh-what?"

"What's that look for? Would it be so bad to date me?" Riley placed her hand on her chest, giving Cam her most earnestly hurt face without breaking into a grin.

For several seconds, Cam's mouth opened and closed like a fish out of water. "No, I didn't say that." She looked down at the floor and unconsciously mumbled, "It wouldn't be bad at all." Cam looked up with panic in her eyes. *Shit, did I really just say that? Do I actually want to date her?*

Riley's eyes widened slightly. "What?"

"N-nothing." Cam said as she shook her head. They both stared at each other, neither one knowing what to say. Just as Riley was about to speak, Cam responded, "I meant what I said last night, Riley. I don't want to lose you."

Riley reached over and squeezed Cam's fingers. "Cam, even if I started dating Bri, which I'm not saying I will. But, if I did, you wouldn't lose me as a friend. You do know that, right?"

"Yeah, I guess," she replied as her gaze returned to the floor.

"Look at me, Cam."

Cam lifted her gaze to Riley's.

"You are one of my best friends. No one could ever replace you."

Cam slowly nodded her head. "Okay."

She wasn't sure if she believed that, but she also wasn't sure if she was only scared of losing Riley's friendship. Deep down she knew her jealousy was stemming from something more, but she still wasn't ready to explore that and didn't know how to put it into context.

"Okay, then. Now, let's go downstairs and make your family some pancakes. Plus, I'm sure you could use some breakfast after throwing up everything you ate last night," Riley said.

Cam scrunched her nose in reply. "Eww. Why did you have to remind me of that?"

"Isn't that what friends are for?" Riley teased as she pulled Cam into a hug.

Cam let out a chuckle and melted into Riley's arms. "Yeah, I guess so."

CHAPTER ELEVEN

Cam spent the next week contemplating the idea of dating Riley. The fact was that she became excited any time she thought about being more than friends with her. It was completely terrifying too. What if she told Riley she had a crush on her only to get shot down? That was a big risk, and one she wasn't sure if she should, or could, take.

Cam sat at their usual lunch table, waiting for Riley to join her. She unpacked a sandwich and apple while keeping her eye on the exit door of the lunch line. Soon Riley stepped into the main room, bringing a wide smile to Cam's face. Just as she was about to wave, she watched as Riley looked behind her and Bri came out as well. Cam stared as they exchanged a few words and flirty smiles. Bri touched Riley's elbow and walked away to her own table. A sense of dread washed over Cam, and she lost her appetite. It wasn't hard to miss the bright smile Riley had on her face as she walked up to Cam's table.

"Hey!" she said as she sat next to Cam.

"Hi," Cam grunted.

"What's wrong?"

"Nothing. Just a bad grade on a calculus quiz."

"That sucks. Was it a big part of your grade?"

"I don't think so." Cam took a bite of her sandwich, only so she wouldn't have to continue lying. She swallowed and it felt like a rock in her as it went down. She didn't have the strength to ask about Bri. Just the thought of them dating made her heart heavy.

She continued to pick at her food while Riley ate and chatted about her morning classes. She replied when necessary but didn't add much to the conversation. They went their separate ways after lunch, but Cam's concentration vanished for the rest of the day. She tortured herself by replaying the way Riley had smiled at Bri.

She found it ironic that just as she was thinking about being more than friends with Riley, Riley seemed to be interested in someone else. Any hope Cam had was slipping away.

* * *

Christmas break came and the holiday itself went by quickly for Cam. She spent several days hanging out with her entire family. Her dad had taken time off work and stayed at their house for five days, and her mom had announced she was cutting her hours even more at the restaurant and only going to work the weekends Cam and her brothers were at their dad's house. They spent their days playing games, singing Christmas songs while baking cookies, and watching movies together. It felt almost normal.

Claire spent the break out of town at her grandma's house, but Riley had been over once or twice to play video games and watch movies. While they continued to hang out, something was missing. Before, everything had felt effortless, but now there seemed to be an elephant in the room—Bri. Cam refused to bring her up. Any confirmation of Bri and Riley dating would be a little too painful, so their conversations over the break were comprised of safer topics like school and what they wanted for Christmas.

Cam knew Claire would be back in town for New Year's Eve, so she called to see what Claire's plans were for that night.

"I'm sorry, Cam. I already made plans with Luke. Do you want me to see if we can add you to our dinner reservation?"

"No, don't worry about it. I'm fine. I'll call Riley, and if she's not free, I'll just hang out with my mom and brothers."

"Are you sure? I don't want you to think I'm abandoning you."

"No, it's totally fine. Have fun with Luke."

"Oh, I will. That is something you don't have to worry about. We'll hang out the next day, I promise."

"Sounds good. See ya."

After she hung up with Claire, she immediately pulled up Riley's number, but she hesitated before she pressed the button. What if she had plans with Bri? Would Riley choose Bri over her? Knowing she wouldn't know until she asked, she took a deep breath and called.

"Hey. I was just wondering if you had any plans for New Year's. Want to come over for another movie marathon?"

"Definitely!"

Surprised, Cam blurted, "You do?"

"Of course I do. Why wouldn't I?"

"Um, no reason. Come over at six, okay?"

"See you then!"

* * *

New Year's Eve arrived and Cam reminded her mom that Riley was staying the night. "Okay. Let me know if you guys need anything. The boys and I will have our own movie marathon until one of us falls asleep, and we all know it'll probably be me first," she said with a wink.

"It definitely will be."

The doorbell rang and Cam found Riley outside wearing the same pajama pants but a different T-shirt than their first movie marathon night. "Hi, let's head upstairs and get started."

"Lead the way. I'm ready to load up on junk food!" Riley exclaimed as they made their way into Cam's room.

Laughing, Cam set out pretzels, popcorn, chocolate chip cookies, and brownies on the bed as Riley picked out their movie lineup. Cam also placed a bottle of water and can of pop on each of the nightstands. Riley had chosen several comedies and one Disney movie as their choices for the evening.

Just as they settled on the bed, Riley's phone beeped. She picked it up with a smile and let out a laugh when she opened up the message.

Curious, Cam asked, "What's so funny?"

Riley typed a reply as she said, "It's just a message from Bri. She was wishing me a happy new year and sent a picture of her and her little sister in pink face masks."

"Oh," Cam replied, dejected.

Riley put her phone on the nightstand and turned to Cam with concern. "What's wrong?"

"Nothing."

"Cameron, I can tell something is. It's written all over your face. You're upset about something."

Sighing, she replied, "Wouldn't you rather hang out with Bri? Doesn't she still want to date you?"

"No, I wouldn't. And no, she doesn't."

"How do you know that? I saw how she looked at you at the party and a few times after that."

"Because we tried and it didn't work. We're better off as friends."

Cam's eyes widened and she grew nauseous. "You went out?"

"Just twice. Neither of us felt anything so we agreed to be friends."

Cam relaxed with relief. "Oh. Are you okay with that?"

Riley looked at her intently. "Yes, I am. Is this why things have been awkward between us?"

"What do you mean?"

"Oh, come on. We hang out but we haven't really talked much. Was it always just about Bri?"

This was it. She could just tell her that she wanted to be more than friends. Instead, she shrugged. "I don't know. Maybe a little. I was afraid you'd abandon me for her like Claire did with Luke." *Way to go, chickenshit.*

"I told you before that wouldn't happen. It's taken too long to break you in as my new best friend, so it'd be wasteful to drop you as soon as I got a girlfriend. Okay?" she said with a wink.

Cam quietly chuckled. "Okay."

She released a slow breath, picked up the remote, and pressed play. As the movie started, they settled back on the bed and propped themselves up with a few pillows against the headboard.

They talked very little throughout the night, but Cam was vaguely aware that they were sitting closer on the bed than they normally would. Their closeness gave her that fluttery feeling again in the pit of her stomach, and she found it difficult to pay attention to the movies.

As the credits rolled on their third movie, Cam yawned and stretched her arms above her head. "We should get ready for bed."

"You're probably right."

They went into the bathroom and shared the sink as they brushed their teeth. Every so often, they snuck quick glances at each other in the mirror. Once they finished, Riley went back into the bedroom while Cam returned all the snacks to the kitchen. She found her mom asleep on the couch with the TV on a low volume and set to the classic movie channel. Her mom looked peaceful, but Cam also knew she was tired. So Cam covered her with the afghan from the back of the couch, turned off the TV, and placed a light kiss to the top of her mom's head before going back up to her room.

Riley was lying on her back and Cam crawled under the covers next to her. As she looked at the clock on her nightstand, Cam realized it was already past midnight. "Hey, we missed ringing in the New Year at midnight." Before she could think about what she was doing, she leaned over and kissed Riley on the cheek. She pulled back quickly and mumbled, "Sorry."

"It's okay." Riley squeezed her hand and whispered, "Happy New Year."

"You too, Riley. Goodnight." Cam turned onto her side facing away from Riley and closed her eyes tightly. *What did I just do?*

* * *

Cam woke up the next morning feeling a weight along the left half of her body. She opened one eye and saw Riley's head resting on her shoulder with her arm draped across Cam's waist, and a leg lying on top of hers. Cam's arm was curled around Riley and resting on her hip. Cam immediately opened both eyes and had a mini freak-out. Once she took a few deep breaths and got over the initial shock, she noticed how nice it felt and wished they could stay like this all day. She fought the urge to stroke Riley's arm and feel her warmth beneath her fingertips.

Before she could dwell on things any further, she whispered, "Riley, we should get up."

Riley's response was to mumble something Cam couldn't understand, grip her waist tighter, and bury her face into Cam's neck, her lips barely brushing Cam's skin. Cam felt a tingling sensation all the way down to her toes. She shuddered and fought to suppress a groan. She just wanted to wrap her arm around Riley tighter, but instead, she said firmly, "Riley."

She started to wake, and once Riley realized she was lying on her, Riley's eyes widened and she bolted upright. "Oh my God! Cam, I'm so sorry. I, um, I'll go." Riley stood and started looking for her shoes.

Cam got out of bed quickly while trying to reassure her. "Riley, it's fine. Don't worry about it." As she made her way around the bed, Cam stubbed her toe on the bed frame. "Ow, shit!" She grabbed the hurt foot and hopped on the other. As she started to fall, Riley grabbed her shoulders to steady her.

"Are you okay?" Riley asked.

Cam nodded, gazing between Riley's eyes and lips as she unconsciously licked her own. Riley's gaze traveled to Cam's lips and her breath hitched. Riley closed the distance between them. It seemed like Riley was moving in slow-motion, as if she wanted to give Cam ample time to stop her if she was going too far. Finally, only inches away from each other, Cam felt Riley's body heat as Riley leaned in and lightly brushed her lips against Cam's.

She looked at Cam tentatively and Cam saw hints of fear and desire. Cam closed her eyes, dropped her hands to Riley's waist, and went in for another kiss. Riley froze and let out a gasp.

It was different. She knew that right away. Riley's lips were soft and sweet, and her slow movements were intoxicating. With the first brush of Riley's tongue against her own, Cam's only conscious thought was that she never wanted to stop.

However, she was running out of breath. She rested her forehead against Riley's, trying to slow her breathing.

Riley whispered, "Wow."

"Yeah, wow," Cam said softly with her eyes still closed. Realizing what just happened, her eyes snapped open, she dropped her hands from Riley's waist, and stepped back abruptly. "Oh, shit!" she said as she retreated farther and ran her hands through her hair.

"Okay, Cam, don't freak out."

"Don't freak out?"

"Please don't."

Out of the corner of her eye, Cam noticed Riley looking at her helplessly while she paced back and forth, wringing her hands, but her concern for Riley couldn't stop her panic.

"Are you okay?" Riley asked.

"No...yes...oh, I don't know." Cam stopped pacing and leaned back against her bedroom door with her hands covering her face.

Riley pulled her hands away from Cam's face, but Cam kept her gaze focused on the ceiling. "Do you regret it?"

Immediately, Cam's mind wanted to say yes but that would be a blatant lie. She looked back at her and said quietly, "No."

A slow smile spread across Riley's face. "Am I the first girl you've kissed?"

Cam nodded.

"The first girl you've been attracted to?"

She shook her head.

"Well, I won't say anything, and we can chalk this up to a one-time thing if that's what you want."

Cam recognized the hope and fear in Riley's eyes because she was pretty sure hers were a mirror image. "That's not what I want, Riley. I think I've had a crush on you since the first time I saw you at the library." After a beat she asked, "What does this mean? I've only dated guys before."

Riley took a deep breath as if she was carefully choosing her words. "I'm sorry, but I can't tell you how you feel or what you want. And you don't have to put a name to this or decide anything right away. We can talk more about this later, but I'm gonna go. I know how it feels to discover you might not be the same person you've always thought you were. I know I had to process it alone first before I really talked to anyone else about it."

Riley packed her things, but she immediately stopped when Cam said in a shaky voice, "Riley...I'm scared."

She crossed the room and wrapped her arms tightly around Cam's shoulders and kissed her temple. "I know. I'm sure this feels confusing, but I'm always here if you want to talk. Remember there's no rush to anything, okay?"

Cam nodded against her shoulder.

Riley cupped Cam's cheeks with her hands and used her thumbs to wipe away the tears that had fallen. "Can I kiss you again?"

Cam nodded with a soft smile.

Riley briefly pressed her lips against Cam's. Pulling back with a smile, she said, "Happy New Year, Cam."

"You too." Then Riley grabbed her bag and headed down the stairs.

After Cam closed her door, she stood there unmoving, reveling in the lingering sensation of Riley's lips on hers. It was a kiss she wanted to repeat. It felt like a kiss full of promise.

After saying a quick goodbye to Cam's mom, Riley walked toward her car in a slight daze. She threw her bag across the console and onto the passenger seat before getting in the car and sitting there motionless for several minutes. *She kissed me back.* She shook herself out of her stupor and drove away before either Cam or her mom noticed she was still in their driveway and came out to investigate why.

As Riley arrived home, she was immediately comforted by the fact that her mom's car was already parked in her spot. She was freaking out and she needed someone to calm her down. She found her mom making coffee and still dressed in scrubs. "Hi, Mom. Just get home?"

Her mom offered a wide smile as she closed the distance between them and pulled Riley in for a hug. "About twenty minutes ago. Happy New Year! Have fun last night?" she asked as she held Riley by the shoulders.

Riley nodded slightly, looked toward the floor, and quietly said, "I did."

Her mom grinned and offered, "Why don't you have a seat and tell me all about it?"

Riley poured herself a cup of coffee and sat next to her mom. "We kissed," she whispered.

"Wait, what? Did you kiss her, or did she kiss you?"

She looked up at her mom with a bashful smile. "I kissed her." She paused and took a deep breath. "But then she kissed me."

"And?"

She released a contented sigh. "And, it was perfect."

"Okay, how did Cam feel about all of this?"

She relaxed into her chair and held her mug. "Well, she definitely freaked out after she kissed me. I was so scared, Mom. I thought I had royally screwed up and she was going to kick me out or something."

"Did she calm down?"

Riley let out a slow breath in relief. "She did. I mean she's still a little freaked, but she said she's had a crush on me since the day we met. I can tell she's still scared, but I think I might have a chance, Mom. I just have to be patient."

Her mother reached over and squeezed Riley's hand. "Make sure you're careful. I don't want you getting your hopes up and your heart broken if she decides she can't handle what all of this would mean for her if you guys got together."

Riley's smile dimmed. "I know." But, she perked up and continued with as much bravado as she could. "Don't worry about me. I'll be fine."

"That's my job, honey. It comes with the territory."

"I know, but I think this could be really good. I just have this feeling it's all going to work out."

Her mom stood and placed a kiss on top of her head. "I hope so," she said. She took her mug to the sink, rinsed it out, and placed it in the dishwasher. "Well, I'm going upstairs to take a shower. Think about what you want for dinner."

"Okay," Riley replied, absentmindedly twirling her coffee cup on the table.

After Riley left, Cam spent a couple hours in her room just replaying the morning. She never would have imagined kissing Riley would feel so right. Her lips had been so soft and comforting and Cam hadn't wanted it to stop.

But every time she thought about how nice it was to kiss Riley, she became confused about what it all meant and what would happen next. She wasn't in complete denial. She could admit that Riley wasn't the first girl she had been attracted to over the years. Before, Cam had just seen cute girls from afar and thought she had just been appreciating their attractive looks rather than thinking about dating them. But with Riley, all of that had changed. Cam had known something was different since the moment she saw her at the library. And since that time, Riley had become her best friend aside from Claire.

Oh shit! Claire! They had made plans to hang out, and Cam had no idea what she was going to tell her. She didn't know if she even wanted to tell her anything. She had never known her to be judgmental, but what if all that changed because she was Claire's best friend and not some stranger? Cam couldn't explain what was going on to herself, so how was she going to explain it to Claire?

She paced back and forth in her room until she heard her mom call up the stairs, "Cam! Claire's here."

"Shit, shit, shit," she muttered. "Be right down." She looked in the mirror and made the decision that she would wait to tell Claire. She hated the idea of lying and hiding this new development, but she hoped Claire would understand why she was doing it, especially since Claire knew she processed things first before letting others in on what was going on.

She took a deep breath before going downstairs. Claire was sitting with her mom in the kitchen. "Morning."

"Well, you finally emerged from your bedroom. I thought you were going to sleep the day away. Did you and Riley stay up late last night?"

She cleared her throat and kept a controlled tone. "Oh, not really. Ready to go, Claire?"

"Yep. I thought we'd go grab some burgers," she said as she stood and placed a kiss on Cam's mom's cheek. "Bye, Ms. Leoni."

"Bye, girls. Have fun."

They got into the car and Cam immediately picked a radio station and turned the volume up loud, to the point where they couldn't talk without shouting. She knew it was an immature move, but if it delayed any talk about her night with Riley, then she was going to do it.

Once they were seated at their table, they glanced at the menu, but this place was one of their favorites, so it didn't take long for either of them to decide. After placing their order, Cam asked, "How was your night? What did you guys do?"

Claire replied with a wide smile. "It was great. We had a really nice dinner, and then went back to my house and watched a movie."

"And, I'm sure you didn't watch much of it."

Claire put her hand on her chest and gasped in mock innocence. "Why, Cameron, I have no idea what you are insinuating."

She let out a snort, and said, "Sure, you don't."

Laughing, Claire continued, "Well, you're right. We didn't watch too much of it." Her gaze took on a wistful, faraway look before she said, "But it was a really nice night."

"I am really happy for you, Claire. I hope you know that."

"Oh, I know, and thank you." The waiter delivered their food and they dug in. Claire asked, "How was your night? What did you and Riley do?"

She instantly felt heat rise to her cheeks which she tried to cover up by wiping her mouth with her napkin. "Oh, we pretty much just ate a bunch of junk and watched movies. It was fun."

Claire narrowed her eyes and asked, "Is that all?"

"Um, yeah." She picked up her burger for another bite, but she wasn't even that hungry anymore. Lying to Claire was making everything in her stomach turn sour.

"Why do you look guilty?" She looked at Cam suspiciously. "You didn't go find a party to hook-up with guys, did you?"

Cam laughed loudly. Maybe too loudly. "Do you really think I'd do that? I think you know me better than that."

Claire joined the laughter, not sensing any awkwardness from Cam's reply. "You're right. That's so not you at all. It doesn't really seem like Riley either, am I right?" Claire finished the last bite of her burger and pushed her plate away.

"Yeah, I don't think she would do that."

"Is she dating anyone? She never really talks about that kind of stuff."

Cam shrugged as she pushed her own plate away. "Oh, I don't think so." She looked out the window to avoid Claire's gaze.

"Does she talk to you about it?"

She cleared her throat and tried not to shift uncomfortably in her seat. "N-no...not really." She was cringing inside, and her stomach was in knots. *Shit, why does she have to ask these questions?*

"I hope she knows she can. She should know that we're trustworthy and always available to talk." Claire looked away briefly before saying, "You also know that too, right? I'm sorry if you've felt neglected lately, and I've been wrapped up in Luke. It doesn't matter what is going on in my life. I will always be here for you."

She averted her gaze and looked down at her hands because she couldn't meet Claire's gaze, knowing she had just lied to her. "Yeah, I know. That goes for you too, you know."

Claire seemed satisfied with that answer, nodding as she asked, "Ready to get out of here?"

"Yeah, let's go."

The drive back to Cam's house wasn't awkward because Claire seemed oblivious to what was stewing inside Cam's brain. Outwardly, she pretended as if nothing was wrong by singing along to the radio, but inside she just wanted to scream and even cry a little.

Claire pulled into Cam's driveway and put the car in park. She gave her a hug, and said, "I'll pick you up on Monday."

"Sounds good."

Cam got out of the car and walked slowly to her front door. When she got inside, she quickly said hi to her mom and brothers before making her way up to her room. She sat down on her bed with a thud, placing her elbows on her knees and her head in her hands. She was already feeling the uneasiness of keeping this huge secret from Claire, and she was terrified of what was going to happen once Claire found out.

CHAPTER TWELVE

On the last night of break, Cam spent most of the evening talking with Riley on the phone. They hadn't seen each other since New Year's but they had talked on the phone extensively every night. She had been helping Cam figure out what all her feelings meant. Since she knew Cam didn't want anyone else to know, she recommended Cam do research on websites aimed toward LGBTQ teens. While not everything Cam found was helpful, it was encouraging to see that she wasn't the only one in the world with conflicting emotions. For once, she had stopped feeling so alone.

After chatting for a few minutes about their days, Cam shifted the focus of their conversation toward more serious and personal topics. She was grateful for any insight Riley could give her into the conflicting emotions she had swirling inside her. So far, no matter the question, Riley had been patient, comforting, and understanding.

"When did you know you were gay?" Cam asked quietly during a lull in the conversation.

"Um, I think it was around seventh or eighth grade. I knew I was different than some of my other friends because I never paid attention to guys except to be friends or play sports and video games with them. And when other girls would talk about their celebrity crushes, I thought about girls instead of guys."

"Have you ever kissed a guy?"

"I have. His name was Derrick and it was during a game of Truth or Dare the summer before eighth grade. Definitely helped cement the idea in my mind that guys weren't going to do it for me. I felt absolutely nothing."

Cam let that roll around in her head a bit. She couldn't say that about the guys she had kissed, especially Danny. A pre-emptive blush rose up her neck and cheeks before she asked her next question. "Have you ever had sex with a guy?"

"No."

"With a girl?"

"Yes."

"Okay then," Cam mumbled. There was so much more she was curious about when thinking about sex between two girls, but her nerves took over. She would just have to file that question away for later. She cleared her throat and asked, "How did you come out? How did your parents and friends react?"

Riley took a deep breath and said, "My friend, Mike, was actually the first person I told that I thought I was gay." She let out a soft chuckle. "He actually asked me to the eighth grade dance, but I had to turn him down. I didn't want to lie and give him the excuse of just wanting to be friends, so I told him I was a lesbian. He was great about it. You could tell he was disappointed. I kinda got the feeling he had a crush on me, but he never said anything bad. I didn't tell my other friends until I started dating Abby. My other friends, Brian and Katie, were great about it too. It didn't even seem to faze them when I admitted Abby and I were dating. I think it helped that we had been a close group of friends for a couple years by that point."

Cam felt an immediate twinge of jealousy when she heard Abby's name. "Did you and Abby date long?"

"Um, we dated for most of junior year."

"What happened? Why did you break up?"

"I guess the big reason was that I knew I was moving and I didn't think we could work that out. But I also knew she wasn't it for me. I love her and she's a great friend, but it felt like something was missing—that there should be something more."

"D-do you still love her?"

"Yes, I love her. I will probably always love her—as a good friend, nothing more. But, I'm not in love with her. You don't have anything to worry about. I really like you, Cam, and I want to see where things go between us if you're up for it."

Cam breathed a quiet sigh of relief. "I definitely am."

"Good. Um, so, coming out to my parents didn't go as smoothly." She let out a sigh. "You know I'm pretty close with both my parents, but my mom especially. I sat her down one day about a month or two after my sixteenth birthday and told her. She kind of just sat there in silence for a few minutes. Once I started crying, she pulled me in for a hug and told me she loved me no matter what. I let her tell my dad, and later he told me that he loved me. But I'll be honest, those first few weeks after I told them were pretty uncomfortable. A couple times they asked if I was going through a phase or if I was just confused. It took a lot of talking to get where we are now. They were great when I started dating Abby and then after we broke up. I know I'm lucky that I can talk to my mom about crushes or girls I'm into, you included."

"Your mom knows about me?" Cam squeaked out.

Riley let out a small laugh. "Yeah, she does. Is that okay?"

"Sure…I guess. I have no idea what my mom and dad are going to say, or Claire. Shit, I feel like it's not going to go well. They'll probably think it's totally coming out of nowhere."

"Don't worry about it too much right now. You're just starting to figure it out for yourself. You can take as much time as you need before letting other people know. Cam, this is your thing. You dictate who knows and when they find out. Okay?"

"Okay."

"And no matter what happens, good or bad, I will be there for you. Even if that means nothing more happens between us. Okay?"

"Okay. Thanks, Riley. That means more to me than you'll ever know."

"You're welcome. Have the websites I sent you helped at all?"

"They have, yeah. I never knew any of this stuff. It's nice to know there are others who feel like I do. I never really saw sexuality as a spectrum before, and it's certainly not talked about in school, at church, or home. I always thought there was just straight and gay. To see others talk about feeling conflicted growing up because they thought both guys and girls were cute, but they didn't know what to do with those feelings has been reassuring. So, seeing that has made me realize I'm not alone. But as soon as I saw the term bisexual and what it meant, I wasn't confused anymore. It all made sense.

"I mean, as a kid, I always felt more comfortable around guys than girls. I refused to wear dresses or makeup and do my hair. I would rather climb trees or play video games than play with dolls or do anything considered girly, but when I felt attracted to others, it wasn't just for the guys I hung around with. Seeing cute girls brought butterflies to my stomach just like seeing a cute guy did." She was quiet for several seconds before asking, "Does that bother you?"

"What?"

"That I'm attracted to guys and have only dated them before?"

"Why would that bother me?"

"I don't know. After reading a bunch of things online, a lot of people seem to be uncomfortable when the people they're dating like more than one gender. There were so many posts about people thinking bisexuals are greedy or cheaters or confused. That's not me, Riley. I want you to know that."

"I do know that. And no, it doesn't bother me. I know there are some people who feel that way, but I'm not one of them. Got it?"

She let out the breath she had been holding and smiled. "Yeah, I got it. Thanks."

"You're welcome. It's getting late, so I should probably get ready for bed."

She looked at her alarm clock and noticed it was close to midnight and they had been talking for a couple hours. "You're right. I didn't realize it was so late."

"Me neither. Guess time just flies when you're talking to a cute girl."

Blushing, Cam replied, "Guess so."

"I'll see you at school tomorrow. Goodnight, Cam. Sweet dreams."

"You too. Bye."

After kissing Riley, Cam hadn't been sure when or if she was going to label her sexuality. All she had known was that she had only dated guys, which could be great, but she couldn't hide the attraction she felt toward some girls, especially Riley. There was no way she wanted to deny that, but telling Riley she was bi felt right, just like it probably felt for Riley when she told Mike she was a lesbian. Cam didn't know how or when she would tell her parents or Claire, but for now, she couldn't think about it. Coming to terms and defining her sexuality was the first step. Exploring what she had with Riley was next. Telling others would happen. Eventually.

CHAPTER THIRTEEN

January was nearing its end, and while Cam kept busy with school and work, she had less responsibility for her brothers since her mom cut her hours at her second job. Cam's free time was spent hanging out with Riley and Claire. She and Riley rarely had one-on-one time, so they snuck kisses at every opportunity but had yet to go on a real date.

On the last Wednesday of the month, they made plans after school to do homework together since Cam had the night off from the library and Claire had plans with Luke. Riley drove Cam home and they went up to Cam's room after saying a brief hello to Ethan and her mom.

Once they closed the door, they tossed their backpacks onto the floor and stood at the foot of the bed shyly staring at each other before Riley cupped Cam's face and closed the distance between them to place a soft kiss on Cam's lips. Cam wrapped her arms around Riley's waist and pulled them together.

Just as Cam opened her mouth wider and teased Riley's lower lip with her tongue, she heard Claire's voice in the hallway,

"Hey, Ethan." Then Claire opened the bedroom door—only a second after Cam and Riley had separated. "Hey, guys." She eyed them both curiously once she noticed they were out of breath. "What have you guys been doing?"

Cam tried not to panic, but she had a feeling she was failing, miserably. Thankfully, Riley stepped in front of her, and calmly said, "Nothing. We were just goofing around. Wanted to delay homework as long as possible, ya know?"

"Uh-huh," Claire replied, her tone laced with suspicion. "I just came over to see if I could borrow your physics notes, Cam."

Cam cleared her throat as she went rummaging in her backpack. "Um, sure. Here you go," she said as she handed over the notebook but kept her gaze averted from Claire's.

"Everything okay?"

She looked up then, trying to look unaffected. "What? Oh, yeah—everything's fine."

Claire's mouth tightened into a thin line. Knowing Claire for all these years meant that Cam could read Claire's facial expressions. And right now, they were screaming that she didn't believe a word of what Cam just said. "Okay. Well, thanks for the notes. I'll give them back to you tomorrow. Bye, guys."

"See ya, Claire," Cam replied as Claire shut the door. Cam sat down on the bed and put her head in her hands. "Shit, she almost caught us."

Riley sat down next to Cam and wrapped her arm around her waist. "I'm sorry."

Cam dropped her hands, turning her head to look at Riley. "You have nothing to be sorry for. I should be the one who's sorry. I'm the one hiding and lying to everyone."

"Cam, you're not lying. You're only just coming to terms with this yourself, and it's your decision as to when you let others know about it."

"I know, but Claire is going to think I've lied to her about this. I'm sorry I'm not ready. I hate that you have to hide as well."

"Stop. If you haven't noticed, I haven't told anyone else that I'm gay either, so I'm in the same boat as you."

"Yeah, I guess, but—"

Riley placed a finger against Cam's lips. "But nothing. When you're ready to tell Claire, I will be there for you. Remember what I told you on New Year's—there's no rush. Okay?"

Cam nodded as she moved Riley's hand away from her lips and interlaced their fingers. She leaned in and placed a tender kiss on Riley's lips. She pulled back slightly so their lips were barely touching and said quietly, "Thanks."

"You're welcome. Now, I guess we should do our homework."

"Well that's no fun."

They sat in relative quiet for an hour, shoulder-to-shoulder, completing that night's homework assignments. While Cam worked on her calculus worksheet, she sensed Riley glancing at her occasionally. Figuring Riley had something on her mind, Cam decided to wait it out and let Riley break the silence.

After a few more minutes, Riley cleared her throat and asked quietly, "Um, Cam?"

"Yeah?" she said distractedly as she finished writing the answer to the problem she was working on. Then she looked up and noticed Riley was picking at a thread on the comforter. She didn't say anything for a moment, so Cam asked, "Everything okay?"

Smiling, she said, "Yeah. Just nervous I guess."

"Why?"

Riley stopped picking at the thread and wrung her hands together. "Do you...do you want to go to dinner with me on Saturday?" She glanced up at Cam briefly before looking down at her hands.

Now Cam fully understood Riley's nervousness, and the corners of her mouth quirked up as she tried to hide her smile. Riley was quite adorable when she was nervous. "Like a date?"

"Um, yeah, a date. I mean, if that's what you want."

"I'd love to."

Immediately, Riley looked up at Cam with a beaming smile as she asked in wonder, "You would?"

Cam reached over to hold her hand and their fingers instantly interlocked. "Of course I would," she replied before leaning in to kiss her. As she sat back, Cam asked, "Why were you nervous?"

Shrugging, she said, "I don't know. Part of me was afraid you'd say no. I mean, we just talked about how much you hate that we're hiding, so I know we won't be able to completely act like a couple. I didn't want to scare you off or have you think I was forcing you into any public situation."

"I'm sorry we can't act like a couple, Riley. I will get there eventually. I promise."

"I know. I'm not trying to pressure you."

Cam cradled her face with one hand and trailed light kisses underneath Riley's chin and down her neck. Cam's efforts were rewarded with a shudder and soft sigh. Once she repeated the trail up her neck, she whispered in Riley's ear, "Thank you for being patient with me." Before Riley could reply, Cam captured her lips and kissed her. "I just want you to know how much that means to me."

Riley smiled and nodded as Cam returned to her homework. Knowing the effect of that kiss, the corners of Cam's mouth twitched upward when she heard Riley take a deep, shaky breath.

"I'll pick you up at seven. Is that okay?"

Cam offered her a bright smile. "That's perfect."

Riley closed her Spanish book and reached for her chemistry notes. She placed her backpack on the floor and moved farther down the bed, so she could lie down and rest her head in Cam's lap. Cam's fingers brushed through her hair, bringing a wide smile to Riley's face.

* * *

Saturday arrived and Cam was nervous with first date jitters. While they would've preferred to dress up and celebrate their first date, Cam wouldn't have been able to explain that to her mother so they opted for simple and decided to head to their favorite burger place. Cam dressed casually in skinny jeans, a long beige sweater, and brown boots. She skipped the makeup and pulled her hair into a ponytail.

She went downstairs to wait for Riley and sat at the kitchen table while her mom and brothers ate dinner. "It's still okay for Riley to spend the night, right?"

"Of course. She's always welcome here."

"Great." She turned her head toward the front of the house when she heard a car door close. "That must be her. We'll be back in a little while." She stood and gave her mom and brothers each a hug from behind. Josh tried to squirm away, but she held him tighter and then ruffled his hair.

Cam reached the door a second after Riley knocked. She wore jeans, brown boots, and a tight, dark green sweater that accentuated her eyes and her curves. Cam admired her before stepping outside and closing the door. "You look great, Riley."

"So do you," Riley replied, giving Cam a kiss on her cheek.

Once they were in the safety of Riley's car, Cam reached across the console and squeezed Riley's hand. She gently pulled her toward her for a quick kiss. "Hi," she whispered.

"Hey there," Riley replied with a smile. "Ready for our first official date?"

"Oh yes!"

They arrived at the restaurant and were seated at a small table against a wall of windows. They quickly placed their orders and sat back to enjoy the night. Cam had to fight the urge to reach across the table to hold Riley's hand, but the table was so small that their knees brushed. It may have initially happened accidentally, but neither one of them severed the contact.

"Thanks for saying yes to the date," Riley said after their dinner arrived.

Cam looked at her with confusion. "Did you think I'd actually say no?"

"I just wasn't sure. But, I'm really happy you said yes."

"Me too."

Once they were enjoying their meal, Riley asked, "How are things with your mom now that she's basically just teaching?"

"It's really good. I feel like a weight has been lifted off my shoulders. I'm not as responsible for Josh and Ethan anymore. Now, I can focus on school...and you," she replied with a wink.

"Plus, Mom has been in a better mood, and I can tell she isn't as stressed as she was last year. I think that's making a huge difference."

"That's great. Have you thought about talking to her about us?"

"I have, but I'm not sure when. I want to wait until we both have more time to process it, like during spring break, but part of me just wants to wait until after graduation. If she reacts badly, then I'll be leaving anyway so we wouldn't have to put up with each other for very long. What do you think?"

"Well, I don't know your mom as well as you, so I can't even guess her reaction. I understand wanting to wait for a time where you can both deal with it. If you think waiting until you're ready to leave for college is best, then I'll support that. Do you want me there when you tell her?"

"No, I think it's something I should do myself. Plus, I don't want her to blame you or think you're the only reason for my coming out."

Riley looked at her with wide eyes. "You think she'd blame me?"

Cam shrugged. "I really don't know, but I don't want to take that chance."

"Okay," Riley muttered as she looked down at her empty plate.

Cam recognized the hurt in her eyes, and she reached under the table and placed her hand on Riley's knee, making slow circles with her thumb. "Hey, I appreciate the offer. You know it'll be better to do it alone anyway. Your mom probably wouldn't have been a big fan if you had someone else there with you when you came out to her."

Riley squeezed Cam's hand. "I know. You're right. I just want to be able to support you."

"Well, once I decide when, just be there for me afterward, especially if it goes badly."

"You don't have anything to worry about. I will be there no matter what," she said with a final squeeze of Cam's hand.

"Thanks, Riley. Ready to get out of here?"

"Sure. Let's go."

After returning to Cam's, they chatted with her mom about their night before saying goodnight and heading up to Cam's bedroom.

Riley grabbed her pajamas. As she lifted her sweater over her head, Cam stopped and stared. Riley's abs flexed as her arms stretched above her head. Cam slowly lifted her gaze, imagining the sight that lay underneath Riley's sports bra. Her gaze traveled north—until her eyes locked on Riley's. She realized she had been caught. Blushing profusely, she turned around to change into a pair of shorts and a T-shirt.

Once they brushed their teeth, Cam asked, "Do you want to just lie around for a while? Maybe watch some TV?"

"Sure," Riley replied as she got under the covers. Cam crawled in next to her and curled up to Riley, putting her head on Riley's shoulder and wrapping her arm around her waist. Riley pulled the tie out of Cam's hair, put it on her wrist, and lazily brushed her fingers through Cam's hair.

Cam turned on the TV and flipped through channels until she found a *Friends* rerun. They lay there in silence for several minutes, relishing the warmth of each other. "I had a good time tonight," Cam said softly.

"I'm glad. Sorry I didn't pick a more romantic place. It was hard to compete with my birthday dinner."

"You thought that night was romantic?"

"Yeah, I guess I did. I mean, I knew it wasn't really a date or anything, even though I hoped it was."

"You did?"

"Of course. I told you I had a crush on you since day one."

"I know."

"Speaking of that night, when you made me blow out the candle on my birthday ice cream, I did make a wish."

"What was it?"

"Well, I guess I can tell you since it came true." Riley slipped her hand under Cam's shirt and caressed the skin just above the waistband of her shorts.

"It did, huh?" She leaned up on her elbow to look down at Riley.

"Yep. I wished that you were my girlfriend."

Cam rose a little more and rested her hand on Riley's abdomen. "Is that what I am?"

"Do you want to be?"

Cam smiled brightly. "Definitely."

"Good. Me too."

Cam laid her head on Riley's shoulder and curled around her. Her cheeks hurt from the wide smile that wouldn't fade. Comfortable silence returned, as did Riley's fingers in her hair.

The show ended, but before Cam could let Riley's touch lull her to sleep, she took a deep breath and slowly released it. Then she quietly asked, "Was Abby the first girl you had sex with?"

"Yes, and the only one."

Cam cleared her throat. "So…what's it like having sex with a girl?"

"Are you talking feelings or mechanics?"

Cam blushed. "Um, both?"

Riley turned and faced her. She brushed a lock of hair behind Cam's ear before trailing her hand down Cam's side and resting it on her hip.

"Well, I haven't had sex with a guy, so I have no comparison. The first couple times we fumbled around a lot because we had no idea what we were doing, but I'm guessing it's the same when both people are virgins. Mechanically, you just do what feels good."

Riley paused and locked eyes with Cam. "Like kissing," she said as she brushed her lips against Cam's.

Cam wrapped her arms around the back of Riley's neck and pulled her closer. She held Riley firmly enough that as Cam rolled onto her back, Riley rolled on top of her and straddled Cam's hips.

Riley broke the kiss and whispered, "And touching." She slowly trailed kisses down Cam's neck as one hand grazed the outside of Cam's breast—and Cam gasped.

She gently lifted the bottom of Cam's T-shirt until it exposed most of her abdomen. Riley skimmed her fingers across

Cam's stomach before peppering Cam's bare skin with warm and tender kisses that made Cam's stomach contract in the most delicious way.

As Riley's lips moved lower, Cam let out a strangled whisper. "Oh God."

Just as Riley reached the waistband of Cam's shorts, she stopped and slid back up, so they were face-to-face again. She wore a mischievous grin and said with a shrug, "Or, ya know, whatever." She leaned down for a final, chaste kiss before rolling off Cam and lying on her side.

Cam lay there, staring at the ceiling and struggling to catch her breath. She turned her head and narrowed her eyes at Riley. "You are so evil."

Riley quietly chuckled. "Sorry."

"I don't know if I actually believe you," Cam muttered as she curled into Riley's side yet again.

Riley laughed again and squeezed Cam's hip in response. "I am. I wasn't trying to get you too worked up. I just think it's a good idea if we wait awhile."

"Okay." Cam paused for a beat and asked hesitantly, "So, that's all there is to it, huh?"

"Hey," Riley said. She placed her hand under Cam's chin and looked her in the eye. "It is. Just talk to me, Cam. I probably won't be able to answer every question, but I'll try. I don't want you to feel pressured when we have sex."

Cam nodded. "So, it's when, not if?"

Riley smiled. "Oh, it's definitely when. You gotta know how much I want you. You're smart, caring, funny, and hot as hell. So, yes, it is most certainly when."

Never one to take compliments easily, Cam blushed with the praise and averted her gaze. "Okay," she muttered again, not knowing what to say.

Riley lightly squeezed Cam's chin until she looked back at her. "Okay, then." Their lips met in a reaffirming and lingering kiss. Riley pulled away and said, "But when we finally do, it's going to be great."

CHAPTER FOURTEEN

When Cam got in Claire's car the Friday before Valentine's Day, Claire asked, "Do you have any plans for Valentine's?"

While she hadn't talked to Riley about it yet, Cam wouldn't have been able to tell Claire that she had plans with her girlfriend, but she would have to play it off as just two friends celebrating being single. "I'm not sure. I'll probably just see if Riley wants to hang out."

"Do you want me to try and find you a date? I mean, you've been broken up with Danny for a while now. You should try dating again," Claire said gently.

"No, that's okay."

"I can find a date for Riley too, if that's what you're worried about."

"Oh, I don't think she likes celebrating Valentine's Day, so I doubt she'd want to do that." Cam looked out her window because she couldn't look at Claire and lie. She honestly had no idea what Riley's feelings were about the holiday, but she needed to avoid going on a triple date. That had disaster written all over it.

"Are you sure?"

"Yeah, I'm sure. You go out with Luke, and Riley and I will hang out if she wants."

"Okay." As Claire pulled into her parking space, she shut off the car, but sat there gripping the steering wheel. "You guys seem to hang out a lot."

Warning bells blared. She knew she had to remain calm and neutral so Claire wouldn't suspect anything. "Yeah, I guess we do."

"That's good," she said a bit curtly.

"Are you jealous?"

"No…okay, maybe a little."

"No offense, Claire, but you haven't exactly been that available lately."

Claire placed her hands in her lap and stared at them. "I know. I'm sorry."

"It's okay. I'm sure I was like that when I was dating Danny." *Just like how I am with Riley now.* Cam cringed inside. She was skirting the truth with Claire and even trying to put the blame back on her. She could see Claire was upset that they hadn't hung out as much lately, but she didn't know whether it would make it better or worse if Claire knew the real reason she spent so much time with Riley. "You really love him, don't you?"

Claire smiled. "I really do. It's crazy, huh?"

"I don't think so. I'm happy for you."

"Thanks, Cam. And, I promise I will get better at finding time to hang out with you. I know I need to make more of an effort, okay?"

"Okay."

Claire gave her a quick hug. "Ugh, let's go get another school day over with."

* * *

For Valentine's Day, Riley and Cam decided not to go out. Since they couldn't openly be a couple, they thought it was pointless to go out on a night made for couples. Instead, Cam invited Riley to spend the night. Cam's mom was working because she knew it would be a good night for tips. Cam also suspected that her mom didn't want to sit at home and think about her divorce.

Because her brothers were also home, Cam opted for video games and junk food. By the time Riley arrived, she and her brothers had set up the living room with the controllers laid out on the coffee table next to bags of chips and pretzels, and cans of pop. Cam opened the door to let Riley in, but checked to make sure her brothers were occupied before gently kissing Riley. "Happy Valentine's Day."

"You too." Riley placed her bag at the bottom of the stairs and took off her coat, hanging it up in the closet. "So, what's the plan?"

They took a seat on the couch with Josh and Ethan sitting on the floor in front of the coffee table. "Eating a bunch of crap while we beat my brothers in *Mario Kart*."

"Hey!" Ethan yelled. "That is so not happening!"

"Bring it on!" Riley said.

For a few hours, Josh and Ethan tried to gang up on Cam and Riley. After a while, they decided to switch it up and Riley moved to the floor to play next to Ethan while Josh joined Cam on the couch.

As Cam watched Riley conspiring and whispering with Ethan, warmth spread throughout her. She was always amazed at how Riley made her feel when they were alone together, but she was equally happy to see her easily getting along with her brothers. Family was extremely important, and having her girlfriend fit into that life made Cam fall for her even more.

Wait. Fall for her? Cam knew she felt strongly for Riley, but she didn't think she could fall in love this quickly. It took her five months to say it to Danny. She was a little scared that her heart was moving too fast.

"Cam, you know you're running into the wall, right?"

She jerked her head up to see that her character was in fact driving straight into a wall. "Oh, whoops. Guess I got distracted."

They finished that round with Josh as the winner. Before he could start another game, Cam said, "It's getting late, guys. Let's clean up and head to bed."

"Oh, come on, Cam," Ethan whined, a clear sign he was also tired.

"No, you guys need to be in bed before Mom comes home. It's already past eleven. Help me clean up this place."

"Fine," Ethan muttered as he shut off the system and put the controllers on a shelf on the TV stand.

They all pitched in and gathered the trash and half-full bags of snacks and took them into the kitchen. With mutters of goodnight, her brothers headed upstairs for bed. Cam made sure everything was neat enough for her mom, and she turned off the overhead light, leaving a lamp on so her mom could see when she got home. Riley picked up her bag and followed Cam upstairs. They took turns getting into their pajamas and brushing their teeth.

As Cam closed her door, she noticed Riley sitting on her bed holding a small box. "Whatcha got there?"

"It's for you."

"What? I thought we weren't getting each other anything."

"I know, but I saw this and thought it would look good on you, so I thought tonight would be a perfect time to give it to you."

"But I don't have anything for you."

"No worries."

Cam sat next to Riley and took the box from her hand. When she opened it, she saw a rose gold necklace with a small crescent moon pendant. She took it out of the box and handed it to Riley. "It's beautiful. Can you put it on me?"

After Riley clasped the ends together, she placed a light kiss on the back of Cam's neck. "Like it?"

Cam held the pendant between her fingers. "I love it. I'm sorry again that I didn't get you anything."

"You're all I need, Cam," she whispered as she leaned in for a kiss.

Cam pulled back with a smile. "Back at ya."

CHAPTER FIFTEEN

Cam thought fall semester was busy, but spring semester seemed to fly by because of everything she had going on. Spring break was only a couple weeks away, and while other seniors had started slacking off, she was trying to maintain her GPA so she wouldn't lose the scholarship she had been awarded by a local business.

On top of that, she picked up more hours at the library to earn extra cash in preparation for everything she needed for college. Claire had also been busy with school, and of course, Luke. Unfortunately, their dating was still putting a damper on Cam's friendship with Claire, and Claire hadn't yet made any effort to hang out more. But Cam couldn't really fault her for it, seeing as she spent most of her free time with Riley.

Since it was Friday, Riley gave Cam a ride home because Claire had a standing date with Luke. They said hi to Cam's brothers in the living room and quickly headed upstairs to her bedroom. As soon as Riley closed the door, Cam gently pushed Riley against it. Her hands traveled up Riley's arms, across her shoulders, and up her neck until she cradled her face, lightly brushing her thumbs over her cheeks. Cam looked into her eyes and whispered, "You are so beautiful."

Riley gave Cam a shy smile as Cam kissed her tenderly, in a way that—she hoped—conveyed how much Riley meant to her. All Cam wanted to do was memorize the softness of her lips and the warmth of her skin. After several minutes, Cam reluctantly broke the kiss, needing to catch her breath, and she leaned her forehead against Riley's.

Cam cleared her throat. "Slow. We're supposed to be going slow. Um, want to watch a movie?"

"S-sure. Your turn to pick."

While Cam looked through all the titles, Riley wrapped an arm around her waist and brushed the hair off Cam's neck, lightly kissing her just below her ear. "I thought we were stopping?" Cam asked with amusement in her voice.

"Sorry. Can't help myself," Riley said softly as she trailed light kisses down Cam's neck.

Cam turned and rested her forearms on Riley's shoulders, burying her hands in her hair.

"You're not sorry at all."

Riley was sporting her knowing grin as she stared at Cam's lips. "You're right. I'm not," she replied in a slightly husky voice as she leaned in for a bruising kiss. Riley grasped Cam's waist and pushed her back, so she was practically sitting on her desk with Riley standing between her legs. Goosebumps broke out across Cam's skin as Riley slowly moved her hands underneath Cam's T-shirt and up her sides. Cam moaned—and they heard a gasp.

"What the fuck?"

They pulled apart and looked toward the door.

"Claire," Cam whispered.

Claire's jaw dropped open as she continued staring. Riley stepped backward and Cam stood and straightened out her shirt, but before she could explain, Claire bolted down the stairs.

"Claire! Wait!"

Cam ran down the stairs, hearing her mom ask Claire if everything was okay. She didn't answer but rushed out the front door. As Cam hit the bottom of the stairs, her mom came up to her with confusion and concern etched across her face.

"What was that all about?" She looked to Cam and then to Riley, who had followed Cam down the stairs, and back to Cam again.

Cam was sure she had that deer-in-headlights look since she was too stunned to speak. Finally, Riley spoke up. "Cam?"

Cam shook her head to clear it and looked at Riley, both of their eyes full of fear. "You should go."

"Are you sure?"

Cam nodded. She watched Riley hesitate and then finally accept the fact that it wasn't a good idea to stay.

"Okay. Call me later." She grabbed her backpack and headed out the door.

"Cam, what happened?" her mom asked as soon as the front door closed.

"Nothing. I'll be upstairs."

She turned to go, but her mom grabbed her wrist. "Oh, no you don't. Go sit in the kitchen. You're going to tell me what's been up with you lately."

Hesitantly, Cam made her way into the kitchen and sat at the table. She couldn't look at her mom, so she just stared at her hands. She was having a hard time processing what just happened. She was trying not to panic, hoping she hadn't ruined her friendship with Claire. Plus, she knew her mom wasn't going to let her leave until she heard the truth, and Cam didn't think she could lie anymore about who she was. Tears stung her eyes before they trailed down her face.

"Cameron, what's wrong?"

"I can't," Cam whispered as she took in a shaky breath.

"Can't what?"

"Mom...I...um..."

"Whatever it is, just tell me," her mother replied, and Cam heard the underlying fear in her voice.

"I'm bi," she whispered. *Holy shit, did I just admit that?* That was the first time she had said it out loud to anyone other than Riley.

"Bi? What do you mean?"

"I'm bisexual, Mom."

Her mom let out an incredulous laugh. "No, you're not."

"Yes, I am. I figured it out a few months ago. In the back of my mind, I always knew I found other girls attractive. I just forced myself to ignore it before, but I don't want to hide it anymore. I can't."

"It's just a phase, Cam. You're still upset about Danny, but you'll get over it and you'll meet some new guys once you get to college."

Now Cam was getting angry. What right did her mom have to tell her how she should feel? She took a couple deep breaths, trying to calm herself so this wouldn't turn into a shouting match. She just wanted her mom to understand. "It's not a phase, Mom," she said as she crossed her arms.

"Cameron, you're young. You don't know what you want. Is this why Claire stormed out?"

Again, Cam avoided her mom's gaze by looking at the floor. "Yeah. She, um, saw me kissing Riley."

"Excuse me? How long has that been going on?"

"I don't know. Not long."

"Cameron Elizabeth! How long?"

"Since New Year's, I guess."

Now it was her mom's turn to look dumbfounded and Cam watched as her mom struggled with any type of response.

"But she's slept over since then," she said quietly, almost to herself. Her mom shook her head and started yelling. "That's it! You're not allowed to see her again, and she won't be sleeping over ever again. You're grounded!"

"What? But we haven't done anything wrong! You've caught me kissing Danny before and I didn't get in trouble!"

"I'm not arguing about this! The only place you're allowed to go is school and work. End of discussion. Now go to your room!"

"You're unbelievable. I did nothing wrong! What happened to you trusting me?"

"Upstairs, now!" Her mom turned away and toward the sink, gripping the counter until her knuckles turned white.

Cam stared at her mom's back as tears rolled down her cheeks. She rushed upstairs to her room and curled up with her head on Riley's pillow, which still carried the scent of her shampoo. Cam grabbed her phone to call Riley and she answered right away.

"Cam, is everything okay? What happened? What'd you say to your mom?"

"I told her I'm bi," Cam whispered, trying to hold back tears. "She told me I can't see you anymore."

"Oh, Cam. I'm so sorry. I'm—"

"I'm not going to let her keep me from you, Riley."

"It's okay. We'll figure it out. What else did she say?"

"She said it's a phase and that I'm too young to know better," Cam barely choked out amongst her sobs. "She said I can only go to school and work."

"I'm so sorry. I'm sure she'll come around. Just give it some time. It was a shock to my parents too when I came out. It will get better. Please believe me."

"I'll try. God, I wish you were here."

"Me too. Um, have you talked to Claire?"

"No, you were the first person I wanted to call. I'll call her later. Maybe it'll give her time to process this." Cam lay there silently until a thought popped into her head and she bolted upright. "Oh my God, Riley! What if she tells people? It could get all over the school and not just for me, but for you too!"

"Whoa, whoa. Calm down. Claire wouldn't do that. She's your best friend. Don't even think about it. But, if for some reason it does come out, it'll be fine. We graduate in a couple months and then we'll be out of there. I don't really care what others will think."

Letting go of the breath she was holding, Cam said, "I know. I just never thought it would go this way. My mom is so mad, and I don't want to lose Claire. I'm not going to lose you, am I?"

"Never."

The sounds of sniffling came across the phone line on both sides instead of words.

"I should get going. All this yelling and crying is exhausting. I think I'm going to take a nap."

"That's a good idea. Call me later, okay?"

"I will. Riley?"

"Yeah?"

"I…I love you," Cam blurted, slightly cringing because she couldn't believe she was telling her this for the first time over the phone.

"I love you too, Cam," she said. "Get some sleep."

"I will. Bye." Cam put her phone on the nightstand, pulled the covers up to her chin, and held Riley's pillow tightly as she began to drift off, hoping her world wasn't falling apart.

* * *

Over the weekend, Cam had tried reaching out to Claire with texts and calls, but they all went unanswered. She hoped Claire had taken the time to cool off.

However, Cam got the hint that Claire was still mad when she didn't show up Monday morning to pick her up for school. While it seemed Claire was avoiding her, Cam knew that couldn't happen once they both got to school. If Claire even showed up. Maybe she'd just skip school altogether.

After a six-block walk to school, Cam immediately went on a mission to find Riley. She craved the comfort and confidence of knowing someone was on her side just so she could get through her day. But as soon as Cam locked eyes with Riley, she could tell Riley was as nervous as she was.

"Hey," Cam said.

"Hi, Cam."

Riley stood ramrod straight and repeatedly clenched her fists, as if struggling not to comfort Cam in some physical way.

"How are you? I'm sorry we didn't get to talk last night. My mom and dad wanted to have a movie night. By the time the movie was over, it was late, and I didn't want to wake you up."

"Wouldn't have mattered since I didn't sleep much." Cam shrugged. "But I'm okay, I guess. My mom and I are avoiding each other."

Taking a deep breath, Cam looked around and made sure no one was listening. It didn't seem like anyone was, but she whispered, "I think the boys know something's wrong. I was trying to do homework last night at my desk. Everything that happened on Friday just kept replaying in my mind. I must've started crying. I don't know if Josh was in the hallway or he heard me from his room, but he came in, didn't say a word, and wrapped me in a hug before he silently walked back out."

"He's a good kid."

"Yeah, he is. I'm going to miss him and Ethan next year." Before she could dwell on it anymore, she cleared her throat and tried to change the subject. She opened her mouth to say something, but quickly closed it because she didn't know what else to say. Instead, she just shook her head and dropped her gaze to the floor.

Riley lightly brushed her fingers against the back of Cam's hand. "Things will be okay, Cam. We'll work through this together."

Cam met her gaze and gave her a small smile. "Thanks. I'm going to try and find Claire. I'll see you later, okay?"

Riley briefly squeezed her hand and said, "Good luck."

Knowing Riley was supporting her gave Cam more strength for what she was about to do. That boost was short-lived, though, and Cam nervously wrung her hands the closer she got to Claire's locker. Claire crouched, pulling out the books she would need for her morning classes.

"Claire, can we talk?"

Claire answered by standing, slamming her locker door, and glaring at Cam for several tense moments until she rushed off toward her first class.

"Shit," Cam muttered as she hung her head and turned in the opposite direction to get to class.

Throughout the day, Cam tried starting conversations with Claire, but Claire refused to even look at her. After the final bell rang, she caught up with Claire at her locker and tried to talk to her once again.

"Claire, please talk to me." Claire gave her a disgusted snort and turned to storm off. Quickly, Cam grabbed her arm to stop her and stepped in front of her. "Please, Claire. I'm so, so sorry."

She slapped away Cam's hand and narrowed her eyes. "Fuck you, Cam." Then she walked quickly down the hall and out the door.

Cam covered her mouth with her hand to hold back a sob. She realized she was still in the hallway when she noticed several kids staring at her with curious expressions. Quickly, she wrapped her arms around her stomach and rushed down the hallway as tears streamed down her face.

Riley saw her and walked alongside Cam. "What happened? Did you try to talk to Claire?"

Cam couldn't even look in her direction. She just wanted to get out of the school and away from prying eyes as quickly as possible. Riley pulled her into an empty classroom. Realizing they were alone, she threw herself at Riley, hugging her tightly and sobbing uncontrollably.

Riley held Cam and rubbed her hands up and down Cam's back. "What happened?" she asked again. Cam answered with more tears. "Cameron, you're scaring me."

After a few more minutes of crying and once Cam caught her breath, she lightly kissed Riley on the cheek and stepped away, wiping her tears away with the sleeves of her sweatshirt.

"I'm sorry. I tried talking to Claire again and she told me to fuck off. She looked at me like she hates me." Cam sat in the chair closest to her with her elbows on her knees and her head in her hands.

Riley knelt in front of her, rubbing small circles on her thighs. "I'm sure she doesn't hate you. What she saw on Friday was a shock. Give her some more time. It's only been a couple days."

With her hands still covering her face, Cam replied in a shaky voice, "But she's my best friend. I can't lose her."

Riley took Cam's hands in her own, meeting Cam's gaze as she did so. "You won't lose her. Just give it time. She'll cool off."

Cam closed the distance and kissed Riley, releasing a sigh as Riley's warm lips settled her racing mind and heart. Cam pulled back and said, "Thank you—for everything."

"You're welcome."

Cam briefly kissed her again. "I should go. I need to get home before my mom does."

Walking outside, they parted with the promise of talking later that night—a comfort Cam desperately needed.

Cam walked into her house and found her brothers were already on the couch in the living room playing video games. She knew she should ask them if they had done their homework or even make a move to sit down next to them and play, but she didn't have the strength to pretend everything was okay.

"Hey guys, I'll be in my room," she said, not waiting for any kind of reply before heading upstairs.

She flopped onto her bed and curled up with Riley's pillow, breathing in her scent, which was starting to fade away. Her mind replayed the hurt and angry look that Claire sported anytime Cam looked at her. She had never seen Claire so mad before, about anything really, but especially at her. Sure, they had disagreements over the years, but Claire had never been so harsh as she had today. Cam was desperate to make things right between them, but she couldn't fathom how to make that happen if Claire wouldn't even talk to her.

She understood the shock Claire must've felt when she caught her making out with Riley. Claire would've been surprised if she caught Cam making out with a guy, and the fact that she was with another girl certainly multiplied the shock times a million. So, it was understandable if Claire needed some time to come to terms with it, but Cam was impatient and scared. They had never gone this long without talking. She desperately wanted to reach out again, but she knew forcing Claire to talk would push her away even more.

Cam must have fallen asleep, because the next thing she knew, she was shooting upright in bed when she heard a knock on her door.

"Yeah?" Cam asked hoarsely.

Ethan opened the door and poked his head in. "Mom said to come down for dinner."

Cam let a small sigh. "I'll be right down."

He went downstairs, leaving the door open behind him. Cam rubbed her face, ran her hands through her hair, and rolled off the bed to head to the kitchen. This would be their first meal together since the argument with her mom. Over the weekend, Cam had chosen to eat in her room or sometimes not at all.

As she sat down at the table, her mom asked in a tense voice, "How was your day, Cam?"

"Oh, just peachy, Mom," Cam replied sarcastically. "My best friend isn't talking to me and I'm not allowed to see the one person I care about outside of school."

"Enough with the attitude, Cameron. You're grounded and there's nothing you can do about it. Now eat your dinner."

Her brothers glanced at each other with raised eyebrows. The desire to ask what was wrong was written all over their faces, but they must've realized it wasn't a good idea and they kept their mouths shut.

Cam tried to eat her dinner, but it just felt like a rock inside her stomach. After several minutes of pushing her food around, she asked, "May I be excused?"

"Fine," her mom replied tiredly.

She got up, cleared her plate, and put it in the dishwasher. She went upstairs to call Riley, because right now, she was the only one who understood.

Riley was sitting at the kitchen table with her parents, pushing her food back and forth on the plate. She knew she had been uncharacteristically quiet all weekend. Her parents tried to engage her in conversation, but she gave one-word answers. Her thoughts were focused on Cam and what she was going through at home. She wanted to help in some way, but she didn't really know how.

Her mom said, "Steve, will you please leave Riley and I alone for a while?" He cleared his plate and placed a kiss on each of their cheeks. Once he was out of the kitchen, her mom reached over to stop Riley's fidgeting with her fork. "What's wrong?"

Riley pushed her plate away, leaned back in her chair, and stared at her hands in her lap. "Cam came out to her mom and it didn't go well."

"What happened?"

Riley looked away, feeling embarrassed and afraid. She knew her mom trusted her, and she wouldn't get in trouble when she related the story, but she still hesitated.

"You know you can tell me, whatever it is."

Riley slowly nodded and took a deep breath. "I went over to Cam's after school on Friday and we were up in her room. Claire walked in, and um, caught us kissing. She ran out of the house. Ms. Leoni saw that and asked Cam what was wrong. I left at that point, but Cam was basically forced to come out to her mom and admit what Claire had seen. Now I'm not allowed to see her anymore." Riley looked up at her mom, tears pooling in her eyes.

Her mom moved her chair closer to Riley and wrapped her in her arms, resting her head on top of Riley's. "I'm sorry, sweetheart."

"What am I going to do?" She hiccuped. She had tried to be strong in front of Cam, but being held in her mom's arms broke whatever resolve she had left.

"You'll just have to be patient. Let her mom come around."

Riley pulled back and wiped her eyes. "I can't let her keep me from Cam."

"Riley, you need to respect her wishes. It's not going to do either of you any good if you disregard her directives and get Cam in even more trouble. You can still see her in school, right?"

"Yeah."

"Is she allowed to use the phone?"

"So far."

"Then, you'll just have to hang on to what you have for now. I'm sure her mom will come around."

"What if she doesn't?"

Her mom took a deep breath. "She will. Do you want me to call her and talk to her?"

"No, I don't think she'd react well to that."

"Well, let Cam know that I will reach out to her mom if she ever wants me to."

"Okay. Thanks, Mom," Riley said as she fell into her mom's arms once more.

"How is Cam handling all of this?"

"Not well. She seemed so dejected at school today. I think she and her mom are avoiding each other so Cam just hides in her room. And Claire isn't talking to her. She's been her best friend for years, and they've never had a fallout like this."

Her mom let out a sigh as she rubbed circles on Riley's back. "I'm sorry. I wish had a solution for you."

"It's okay. Listening was enough. I'm going to head upstairs and finish my homework."

"Okay, honey. Love you."

"Love you too."

Once Riley was in her room, she opened her chemistry homework, but she couldn't focus on the words in front of her. She hated seeing Cam so defeated and in pain, and she felt utterly helpless. She knew Cam was strong, but feeling shunned by your mom and best friend would be too much for anyone. She could only hope that at least one of them would come around sooner rather than later. Until that day, Riley was going to do whatever she could to ease Cam's pain.

CHAPTER SIXTEEN

Early the next week, following her shift after school at the library, Cam got home in time to grab a quick snack before starting on her homework. She walked in the door to find her mom watching TV in the living room.

"Hey, Cam. How was work?"

They still hadn't had a real conversation about Cam's sexuality. Actually, they had yet to have a real conversation about anything.

Avoiding eye contact, Cam went into the kitchen to grab some pretzels and a pop as she answered, "Fine. I'm going to my room to study."

"Is that all you're eating?"

"Yes."

"You should eat more than that."

"Yeah, well I'm not really hungry, Mom. I'm fine."

Her mom dropped her head to the back of the couch and rubbed her forehead with one hand. Cam briefly considered talking with her, but she was still pissed off, so she went upstairs instead.

As she passed Josh's room, she heard, "Cam?"

Turning around, Cam went into his room to find Ethan and him sitting on Josh's bed.

"What's up, guys? Ethan, it's getting late and you should be getting ready for bed. Josh, did you finish your homework?" Even though she wasn't as responsible for her brothers as she used to be, she still couldn't break the habit of checking on them.

"Yeah. We...we wanted to talk to you," Josh said hesitantly as he looked up at her quickly before staring at his hands.

Cam put her snacks on his desk and grabbed the chair and turned it around to sit in front of them. "Okay—shoot."

They briefly glanced at each other before Josh asked, "Why don't you watch movies or play video games with us anymore? We asked Mom and she said you're just confused right now and working through some stuff."

Clenching her jaw tightly and curling her hands into fists, Cam took a couple of slow, deep breaths as she tried to tamp down her anger, but she knew her anger and annoyance with her mom wasn't what they needed to hear. Instead she focused on the sad truth that she had unknowingly hurt them by shutting herself away.

"I'm really sorry, guys. She's right that I've been dealing with some things, but I'm not confused about anything." She stopped to consider how much they should know and what their reactions would be. She decided honesty was the best policy. "So, you guys like Riley?"

Right away, Ethan smiled. "Definitely. I like her. She showed me a secret shortcut in *Mario Kart*." He scrunched his eyebrows and frowned as he asked, "Why doesn't she come over anymore?"

"Well, that's where it gets a bit complicated." Cam sat back and rubbed her sweaty palms on her jeans repeatedly. "I like her too. I really like her. Um, she's actually my girlfriend." They furrowed their brows as they tried to work this out in their heads.

"Like the way Danny was your boyfriend?" Josh asked.

"Yep."

"But she's a girl," Ethan said in a puzzled tone.

Briefly smiling, Cam replied, "That she is, but that doesn't mean I can't date her."

In his innocent way, Ethan shrugged and said, "Whatever. Can she come back to show me more tricks?"

They heard their mom yell up the stairs to Ethan that he should be in bed.

He jumped up quickly, gave her a hug, and said, "Crap. Night, guys."

Cam watched him go and couldn't help but think, why can't everyone accept it that easily? Turning back to Josh, she saw him still looking at his hands and with the look on his face that he got when he was trying to work out a tough homework problem.

"Josh, are you okay?"

"So, you're gay?"

Although not completely surprised by his question, Cam was thrown off by his matter-of-fact delivery, so she decided she should be just as blunt and honest with him. "No, I'm bisexual. It means my attraction to someone has nothing to do with that person's gender. Does that weird you out?" she asked hesitantly.

He tilted his head to the side before answering. "I guess not. I thought there was just straight and gay," he said.

Cam wanted him to understand, but she didn't know how detailed she should be with her explanation. She didn't want to treat him like a child, but she didn't want to confuse him either. Hell, she was still learning and still felt ignorant about some of the nuances of sexuality.

"I used to think so too. But there's really a whole range for attraction and sexuality. Some people are only attracted to one gender. Some are equally attracted to any gender. Some are attracted to any but still have a preference. And some are attracted to no one at all."

Cam followed his gaze as he looked toward the floor while gripping his sheets as he slowly nodded his head. "Okay, but, why are you crying all the time?"

She took in a swift breath and her head snapped up as she looked at him in surprise. "What?"

"I can hear you through the wall sometimes, Cam."

Cam hated that she was putting her brother in the same position that she was in when she would hear their mom crying after the divorce. She didn't want to give Josh anything more to worry about. She decided not to tell him that their mother had banished Riley from the house. She didn't want him to get caught between their mom and her.

"I'm sorry, Joshie. It's been rough dealing with these feelings and what it means for me. While I'm not confused, it's still scary to wonder how others will react. And Riley and I haven't seen each other much."

"Why not? Is she not treating you right?" he asked with a protectiveness that reminded her of the night when he came into her room to give her a hug when she was crying at her desk.

"She treats me perfectly," Cam said with a smile. "I'm really okay, Josh. It's just been a tough couple of weeks. Okay?" He slowly nodded his head. "Now, I need to go do some homework and you should probably get ready for bed before Mom gets mad. Get your butt up and give me a hug." They stood so she could give him a hug. "I love you."

In his younger brother way, he replied, "Yeah, yeah," but she knew he felt the same because she could feel his arms tighten around her a little more. Pulling away, he said, "Night, Cam."

Cam lightly swatted his arm as she said goodnight and headed into her room. Sitting on her bed, she smiled with pride as she thought about how lucky she was to have Josh and Ethan as her brothers. Even though she often just saw them as kids, she was often amazed by their insight and compassion. She just wished her mom could be as accepting as them.

The following day at school was typical. She had made plans for Riley to come to the library during her shift that night so they could talk and hang out. After her last class, she stopped at her locker. Then she saw Claire walking toward her. Claire had her head down because she was looking at her phone. She finally raised her head and stood still once she met Cam's gaze. It had been a little over a week since Claire had delightfully told Cam to fuck off. Since then, they had avoided each other as much as possible.

When they were about twenty feet apart, Cam could see Claire's eyes were searching for something—maybe something to say or maybe a way out of the situation. Cam decided not to say anything. She wanted to give her time in case she wanted to talk. But that didn't happen. Claire closed her eyes, shook her head slightly, and walked past her without looking at her again. Cam watched her until she entered a classroom at the end of the hallway. Dropping her head, Cam continued outside. She didn't want to be late for work.

Riley arrived at the library about an hour after Cam's shift had started. Cam had texted which section she'd be working in, so Riley went up to the second floor and searched the rows until she found her. Cam didn't notice her and continued putting books back in their rightful spots. Riley took the opportunity to study her beautiful girlfriend. Today she was wearing skinny jeans, black Converses, and a red and black plaid button-down shirt.

She'd learned the little quirks that made Cam who she was. Riley could detect the subtle differences in her expressions which telegraphed her mood—shyness in the forms of a small smile or a hand rubbing the back of her neck—happened any time Cam was complimented or praised. Other times, teasing Riley brought a mischievous glint to Cam's eyes. And when they were alone, Riley became breathless with just one look from Cam.

Before Cam could notice her, Riley looked around to make sure no one was in the immediate vicinity. She wrapped her arms around Cam's waist and kissed her just below her ear.

"Hi, Cam."

Instantly, Cam released a sigh and leaned back into Riley's embrace, and Riley squeezed Cam a little tighter. The feeling of warmth and comfort Riley always got when she had her arms around Cam was short-lived when Cam quickly straightened and looked around frantically.

"I'm sorry."

Sighing, Riley said, "It's okay, Cam. But there isn't anyone around. I wouldn't have done that if there were."

"I know," Cam replied as she looked toward the floor.

Riley placed two fingers underneath her chin. Once their eyes met, she gave her a faint smile and stepped away until her back was resting against the shelves behind her.

"How was the rest of your day?"

"It was fine. Claire and I had a bit of an interaction. We had a slight stare down in the hallway after school. I think I saw less anger in her eyes than I have in a week, but I don't know. She still didn't say anything. Just walked past me without any other acknowledgment." Shrugging with a sad smile, she added, "I guess that's an improvement."

"I know this all sucks. Do you want me to talk to her?"

"No!" Cam looked around again before lowering her voice. "Sorry, no. This is my thing to deal with. Maybe I'll get her to come around eventually. Like you said, I just need to give her time."

"Okay."

Riley struggled not to reach out and offer some sort of physical comfort. It was in times like these that all she wanted to do was wrap her arms around Cam and tell her everything was going to be okay. She had hoped Cam would have relaxed more now that all the important people in her life knew they were together, but she understood why Cam got scared about strangers seeing them from time to time. Riley would never admit this to Cam, but she was still nervous that everything would be too much for Cam, and Cam would break up with her.

After some awkward moments of silence, Riley spoke up. "I should get going. I don't want to get you in any trouble. Plus, I have some homework to do. Can I call you later?"

"Of course. You can always call me."

Cam took a deep breath and looked around once more before gently cradling Riley's face in her hands. Riley relaxed into the touch, closing her eyes to revel in the warmth and softness of Cam's fingertips as they slowly caressed her cheeks. She kept her eyes closed as Cam's lips captured her own. The kiss was slow and settling, and it wiped away all of Riley's fears, for she was able to confirm exactly how Cam felt from this one kiss. She knew she was loved.

Cam pulled away and whispered, "I'll talk to you later."

Riley nodded, and as she turned down the aisle, she felt Cam's gaze on her back. Just as she was about to go out of Cam's field of vision, she glanced back and gave Cam a smile and a wink, happy to see Cam respond with a wide smile of her own.

* * *

It was the end of the school day. Claire and Cam were the last ones to gather their things. As their physics teacher walked out of the room, Cam hurried to close the door to the classroom and she stood in front of it like a guard.

"Get out of my way," Claire growled.

"No."

"What do you want, Cameron?" Claire asked harshly.

"I just want you to talk to me. You can't avoid me forever."

"Why not? You're a liar. I can never trust you again."

"Please, Claire. Let's just talk about this."

"There's nothing to talk about. You disgust me. You and Riley disgust me. Your lies disgust me. Don't talk to me ever again. We're done! Now get the hell out of my way!" she yelled as she grabbed Cam by the shoulders and pushed her to the side. Cam tried to grip the doorframe to keep herself upright, but she missed and crashed to the ground.

Bolting upright in bed, Cam placed a hand on her chest and calmed her breathing. Never had a dream felt so real before. She guessed her little interaction with Claire earlier had been the catalyst for the nightmare. Looking at the clock, she saw it was two in the morning. She extracted herself from the sheets that had twisted around her legs, deciding a drink might help her go back to sleep. She ventured downstairs for a glass of water.

As she reached the bottom of the stairs, she heard what she thought was crying and sniffling. Confused and scared, she tiptoed toward the noise coming from the kitchen. As she peeked around the entryway, her mom sat at the kitchen table with her elbows resting on the table and her head in her hands, her fingers gripping her hair.

Cam was shocked. She had only heard her mom crying throughout the divorce—she'd never seen it. Just as she was about to turn around and head back upstairs, she heard her mom talking to herself and slowly shaking her head from side to side.

"Shit, she could get hurt. People suck. They're mean, they're judgmental, they're…damn it," her mom said a little louder as she rubbed her hands over her face. Her mom must have sensed her there because she raised her head and looked directly at Cam.

Cam noticed her mom's current deer-in-headlights look mirrored the one she gave her the day she came out. "Mom?"

Her mom straightened in her chair, wiped away her tears, and crossed her arms. "Cameron, it's late. You should be in bed," she said in a harsher tone than Cam expected. Cam flinched briefly and opened her mouth to say something, but her mom interrupted her before she could get anything out, and said hoarsely, "Go."

Nodding her head, Cam headed back upstairs as her mom released a heavy sigh. Once she was in her room, she sat on the side of the bed with her elbows on her knees and her head in her hands. She didn't know if she had ever seen her mom so distraught. When her parents were going through the divorce, her mom's expressions were filled more with anger and disappointment. Just now, Cam saw her body language and facial expressions filled with sadness, confusion, and worst of all, fear.

Knowing she was the cause filled Cam with almost overwhelming dread, yet there was a sliver of hope there as well. Maybe her mom was just scared about how others would treat her. Maybe she didn't actually have a problem with her sexuality.

Yeah, right. She barely acknowledges me beyond asking about my day. She didn't really seem to care.

When Cam woke the next morning, she found her mom sitting at the kitchen table drinking coffee. Cam saw the red tint to her eyes and the dark circles surrounding them. Quietly she prepared her breakfast as her mom cleared her throat.

"Have any tests today, Cam?"

Cam looked at her mom as if she had grown two heads, and asked, "Are we really not going to talk about last night? Why were you crying?"

"It's nothing. I guess stress has been catching up with me."

"The stress that I've caused, right?"

"Just give me time. I never expected any of this. I'm not sure what the proper protocol is for any of it."

"And you think I do?" Cam asked incredulously. "Well, I'm sorry I'm such a disappointment and causing you all these problems." She stood, her appetite suddenly gone, and gathered the bowl of untouched cereal to take it to the sink.

Her mom lightly gripped her free arm, looked her in the eyes, and quietly said, "Cameron, you could never be a disappointment. This has just been surprising. I talked with your father and he agreed to have you come and visit during spring break. He'll pick you up on Saturday."

She opened her mouth to say something comforting, but instead she grasped onto the anger she still had inside and said in calm, yet detached voice, "I get it. You just want me out of your sight. That's what you mean by giving you time."

"That is not at all what I meant, and you know it."

"Whatever. I need to get ready for school." Cam put her bowl in the sink and hurried upstairs to get dressed. It seemed avoidance had become her go-to strategy lately, and it must be her mom's as well.

CHAPTER SEVENTEEN

Just as her mom had said, Cam's dad arrived around noon on Saturday to pick her up. Her mom answered the door while Cam finished gathering her things, and she observed how her parents interacted with each other. As time had passed, they had been getting along more and they sometimes seemed genuinely happy to see each other. Today, she didn't know if this was because her mom wanted to see him or because he was taking Cam with him, so they could have a break from each other.

But Cam was happy to see her dad. Her mom had obviously not explained why she wanted Cam to spend the week with him as he never asked about it during their calls. She certainly didn't bring it up either. She already had one parent avoiding her, she didn't want it to be both.

When she saw him at the door, she gave him a tight hug. However, her mood turned slightly sour as her mom offered her a hug and said, "Have a good time, Cam."

Cam stiffened, but she said nothing, trying to be a dutiful daughter. Quickly ending the embrace, she grabbed her bag, put it in her dad's SUV, and climbed into the front passenger seat.

Before she could distract herself with her phone or music, he said, "It's really good to see you, Cam."

With a small smile, Cam replied, "You too, Dad."

He backed out of the driveway and they started their two-hour drive to Cincinnati. After a couple minutes of silence and once they merged onto the highway, he said, "Is everything okay? While I'm thrilled that you're staying with me for the week, it was kind of an abrupt plan. Are you and your mom fighting?"

"You could say that," Cam replied as she picked at a hangnail on her thumb.

"Want to tell me about it?"

"Not really."

"Cam, whatever it is, it's probably not as bad as you think. You can—"

Cam turned to look at him. "You don't know that. You're not there." She watched as pain quickly flashed in his eyes before he schooled his features again. *God, I'm an ass.*

Her dad quietly replied, "I know. And I am sorry for that."

"No, Dad, I'm sorry. I shouldn't have said that."

"It's okay. I know how you meant it."

Cam clenched her jaw, angry at herself for lashing out like she did. Her dad didn't deserve that. She knew she would have to tell him about Riley, but she didn't want to hurt him even more. She released a breath and turned to face him again. "Can we talk about it later? I just don't think I can right now."

"Whenever you're ready."

Cam nodded and then put in her earbuds. She leaned her head against the window, watching the landscape go by. For the next two hours, she had time for her own thoughts and to figure out how she was going to tell her dad that she was bi.

Her father had always been a quiet guy when it came to personal subjects. He didn't necessarily shy away from difficult topics, but he chose to listen instead of offering an opinion or giving advice about things he didn't completely understand. They had never had any deep conversations about Danny or any of the other guys she had briefly dated, although, he had seemed to like Danny.

So it wasn't surprising that sexuality had never come up in a conversation with him before—just like it had never come up with anyone else in her life until recently. Because of this, Cam didn't know what her father's stance was on sexual orientation. Thankfully, she had never heard him saying anything homophobic or intolerant about the LGBTQ community, but she had never heard him say anything in support of them either.

Her dad turned into his driveway and shut off the car. Reluctantly, she pulled out her earbuds and stashed them in her pocket.

As she reached for the door handle, he said, "I was thinking we could get pizza for dinner. That sound good?"

"Sure," she mumbled as she grabbed her stuff and headed for his front door. As soon as they were inside, she started up the stairs. "I'm going to unpack."

Letting out a sigh, he replied, "Okay. Let me know if you need anything."

She walked into her room, threw her bag on the floor, and flopped onto the bed as she started to wonder how long this week would feel. She knew her dad wouldn't necessarily pressure her to talk to him, but he would still ask questions. She just needed to find the strength to answer them. With one arm resting above her head and her fingers twirling strands of hair, she texted Riley, who was spending spring break visiting family and friends in Illinois.

Well I'm here...

She stared at the ceiling and waited for Riley to reply.

Can't be that bad.

Most awkward car ride ever.

Just talk to him. Make him understand.

Easier said than done.

I know. Sorry. I have to head out and meet some friends so ttyl. Love you!

Love u too

Dropping her phone to the bed, she curled up on her side, thinking about what she wanted to say to her dad...

Cam awoke to a knock on her door, as her dad opened it slightly and poked his head inside.

"Cam, the pizza's here. Come on down."

Turning on her back, she rubbed her eyes and said, "Be right there."

He left and she heard the stairs creaking as he went downstairs. She sat up and ran her hands through her hair. After giving herself a few minutes to wake up, she joined him in the kitchen. She grabbed a plate and a couple slices of pizza and sat across from him.

"All unpacked?" he asked.

"No, I fell asleep right away. I'll do it after I eat."

"No rush. Tomorrow I have to go into work in the morning for a couple hours, but then I'm free the rest of the week."

"Okay," she muttered as she continued to eat.

After several minutes of awkward silence, he mused, "You must get that from me."

"What?" she asked.

Pointing to the way she was eating her pizza, he said, "Taking off the pepperoni and eating that first before the rest." He held up a slice of pizza that was already missing its pepperoni. "Guess that's one of many things we have in common."

Meeting his gaze and letting a small smile take hold, she replied, "Guess so, Dad." Maybe this would be as good a time as any to tell him. Not that this was something she'd have in common with him. Just that maybe he'd still think of those positive aspects even after she told him. *Shut up brain and just do it.*

She tossed the crust in her hand onto her plate and slid the plate to the side. She took a deep breath and slowly let it out. Looking up to meet her dad's eyes. "I think I'm ready to tell you now."

He wiped his mouth with a napkin, pushed his plate away, and folded his hands on the table. With an encouraging smile, he replied, "Okay. Go for it."

Her hands trembled slightly so she moved them to her lap. Making eye contact was difficult so she stared at the table as she spoke. "Mom sent me here because I told her something about myself that she doesn't like. I-I'm bisexual. And Riley's my girlfriend." She flicked her eyes up but quickly returned them to look at the table.

Her dad sat in silence before calmly asking, "And how long have you two been together?"

"A few months, I guess."

"How long have you thought that you're, um, bi?"

"I didn't really know the term until after being with Riley. But I think I've always known that I was attracted to more than just guys." She looked up to see her dad nodding his head as if he were trying to process the information.

"I see. Does this have anything to do with your breakup with Danny? I know that was probably hard."

"God, why does everyone think that? No, he has absolutely nothing to do with this," she replied as she sat back with her arms folded.

"I'm sorry. This is just new for me. And your mom. You've never even hinted before about liking girls or anything like that. I mean…I know there are more gay characters on TV and issues about it in the news. It's the popular trend nowadays. I don't know if that has—"

"A trend? It's called visibility, Dad. It makes people, like your daughter, for instance, feel less alone. You have no idea how hard all of this has been for me. To have Claire, Mom, and now you make me feel less because I'm in love with another girl. Why can't you guys just be happy for me?" She wiped a tear from her cheek.

Her dad held up his hands in surrender. "Okay, okay, I'm sorry. Honey, we do love you and that will never change. This is just something we never expected of you. But I just want you to make sure you think carefully about this. I want you to be safe. Choosing to live this way will be difficult and we don't want—"

"Jesus, Dad, it's not a choice! Do you think I want my best friend to hate me? Or for you and Mom to look at me differently now? Do you think I like worrying about who might see me if I hold Riley's hand for too long or I give her a kiss? All I want is to love any person I want, and for everyone else, especially those who supposedly love me, to be okay with that."

"Cam, that's not what I meant. Your safety—"

"I don't want to talk about this anymore." She quickly stood, almost knocking her chair over in the process. Rushing upstairs, she heard her dad calling for her to come back and talk, but she ignored him until she was again lying on her bed and wishing the week could just be over.

Only a few minutes later, her dad knocked on the door but didn't open it. "Cam, please open up so we can talk."

"I can't. Not right now. Just let me be. Please."

He stayed quiet for several seconds. "I don't like it, but okay. I do love you, Cam. Never doubt that."

She didn't reply, but after a moment she heard him walk down the hallway. Eventually, she got ready for bed, even though it was barely past eight. She tried to call Riley, but it went straight to voice mail. She decided not to leave a message because she didn't want Riley to hear how upset she was and feel guilty for missing her call. Curling on her side, she looked at a picture on her phone of them and whispered, "I miss you, Riley." Closing her eyes, she let the tears fall onto her pillow until she fell asleep.

As Riley drove to the bowling alley to meet her friends, she couldn't help but feel badly about having fun when Cam was having such a rough time. She would take away all of Cam's pain and troubles in an instant if she could. She knew Cam wouldn't want her to feel guilty, so she was trying to focus on her night with her friends.

Riley was also meeting Abby's new girlfriend, Sara. Riley hadn't talked to Abby that often over the past few months, but she didn't feel slighted. They were both busy with school, friends, and their girlfriends.

The bowling alley was surprisingly full, so it took her a little while to find her friends at the last lane. Mike, tall and solidly built from football, was the first one to see her and he immediately wrapped her in a crushing bear hug. Next, Brian stepped up and she saw how happy he was by his bright blue eyes and wide smile. Katie had always been the quiet one of the group so she hugged Riley tightly and whispered that it was good to see her. Finally, she stood in front of Abby and was struck by how much she missed her. She gave her a hug before Abby stepped aside and motioned toward a seemingly shy, but gorgeous girl with black hair, dark brown eyes, and light brown skin.

"Riley, this is Sara. Sara, this is Riley."

Riley extended her hand and said, "It's nice to meet you, Sara. Sorry you have to deal with this one."

"Hey!" Abby said as she playfully shoved Riley's shoulder.

"Okay, okay," Mike said. "Let's start. Riley, want to team up with me?"

"Sure, let's do this."

As they started the first game, they quickly got into a rhythm of bowling, chatting, and general razzing on each other. Talking in person seemed to get her more details about their lives than when they talked on the phone or online. She was able to catch up with all the big events she had missed, and she was thankful to have small one-on-one chats with each of them, especially Sara. It didn't take long for her to see how well she and Abby were suited for each other.

When the first game was over, Abby sat down next to Riley. "So, still liking Indy?"

"I am. It's a really great city."

"How's Cam?"

Riley replied with a shrug.

"What's wrong?" Abby asked.

"She's just having a really hard time at home right now."

"How about we go get some snacks for everyone?"

"Sure."

They collected everyone's order and Abby whispered in Sara's ear and gave her a quick kiss on the cheek. Once their order was placed, they grabbed a table to wait for it.

"So, now do you want to tell me what's wrong?"

"Cam came out to her mom, and she's not taking it well. She's also staying with her dad this week and plans to come out to him too."

"Ah—that sucks."

"Yeah," Riley said as she ran her hand through her hair. She explained everything that had happened since Claire caught them making out, and how it was affecting her and Cam. "Sometimes, I just don't know what to do for her. We only see each other at school, except for when we try to sneak off for a few minutes while Cam is at work. I love her so much, but I hate to see her in so much pain." Riley looked at Abby after she realized what she had just said. "I'm sorry if that's weird for you to hear, Abby—that I'm in love."

Abby gently gripped Riley's forearm. "It's not weird at all. You're still one of my best friends and I'm really happy for you. And, I'm kinda in the same boat."

That news brightened Riley considerably. "Oh yeah? You and Sara are pretty serious?"

"Yeah," Abby replied sheepishly. "She's awesome."

"Well, I haven't gotten a chance to talk to her much, but she seems great. I'm happy for you too, Abby."

"Thanks. Look, I know you're unsure about how to handle everything with Cam, but all you can do right now is be there when she needs you and support her."

"I know. That's my plan."

"Good." Just then their order was called. "Let's go."

Abby and Riley gathered all the snacks and drinks on trays and headed back to their lane.

They bowled for a couple more hours and then hung out at Abby's house for a while before Riley headed back to her grandparents' house. After changing into her pajamas, she lay in her bed and pulled out her phone. She noticed she had a missed call from Cam, but there wasn't a voice mail. She looked at the clock and realized it was close to midnight. She knew Cam hadn't been sleeping well lately so she didn't want to risk waking her. Instead she took one last look at a picture of the two of them on her home screen.

"Love you, Cam."

The next morning, Cam woke up after a night of restless sleep. She had tossed and turned because her mind wouldn't stop thinking about how messed up everything was with her mom, dad, and Claire. A call from Riley interrupted her thoughts.

"Hello," she answered a bit groggily.

"Hey, Cam. Did I wake you?"

"No, I woke up a few minutes ago. How was your night?"

"It was a lot of fun. Hung out with a few friends from my old school. We went bowling and then went back to Abby's house and mostly just talked. I was able to catch up with everybody and hear their plans for after graduation. I saw you called. Why didn't you leave a voice mail? I would have loved to hear your voice."

Clenching her jaw and knowing about Riley and Abby's past together, Cam tried to stay calm as she said, "Didn't want to ruin your night. Seems you had fun. Glad you got to hang out with your ex-girlfriend while I had to come out to my dad."

Sighing, Riley replied, "Cam, don't be jealous of Abby. We are friends and nothing more. I love you, I'm with you, and that's not going to change. You know that, right?"

"Yeah," she muttered.

"So…how'd everything go with your dad?"

"Not great, although not as bad as it did with my mom. He didn't yell at least. He told me that I need to think about what I'm doing. He made it sound like I'm with you because being gay is the trending thing right now. Like I would do this because I want to seem cool and want attention. What a bunch of bullshit."

"My parents said something similar to me. You have to give him time to understand. You need show him you're the same person you always have been. He's not going to change how he feels overnight. You and I both wish that were the case, but it doesn't work like that."

"I know. I just wish he and Mom and Claire knew how much all of this sucks for me. I know it was a surprise to everyone, but I just want to be selfish right now and have everyone be okay with it." She took a deep breath to calm herself. "Enough about me. What are you up to today?"

"Oh, um, just going out to lunch with some people. I'm having dinner with my parents and grandparents tonight."

Cam could hear a slight hesitation when Riley mentioned her lunch plans, so she asked, "Who are you going to lunch with?"

"Probably Mike, Brian, Katie, and Abby."

Under her breath, Cam mumbled, "Of course it's Abby."

"Cameron, don't be like that."

Indignantly, she said, "Like what?"

"Jealous. It's not a good look for you." Cam sat on the other end of the phone in silence, so Riley continued. "I know you're having a hard time right now, but you don't need to take it out on me. You trust me, don't you?"

"Yeah, sure."

"Wow, way to sound convincing. Look, I need to go. I'll talk to you later. I love you."

Cam must have hesitated too long because she heard Riley sigh right before she hung up. Cam tried to call her back right away, but she didn't answer so Cam texted her instead.

I'm sorry. I was being an ass. I love u too. Please don't forget that.

She held her head in her hands with her fingers laced in her hair. She sat like that for a moment before she muttered, "Fuck."

After hanging up on Cam, Riley tossed her phone on the nightstand and lay back on her bed with a groan. *What the hell is Cam's problem?* She couldn't understand why Cam had been so bitter and jealous. It was so out of character. She got that things with her parents were shitty, but that wasn't an excuse to act like a jerk. Looking at her watch, she saw she had two hours until Abby picked her up for lunch. So instead of sitting around on her ass and moping about how Cam was acting, she got dressed and headed outside for a long run to clear her head.

As she rounded the first block, she focused on her breathing and her surroundings. Her grandparents lived close to a park that had a nice balance of paved paths and dirt trails, and it had always been one of her favorite places to run.

She settled into a nice rhythm, but her focus shifted toward Cam instead of her breathing. *Why did she react like that?* She knew they would have arguments at some point in their relationship, but she had never given Cam any reason not to trust her.

She made one lap on the two miles of paths that surrounded the park before heading inward and onto the trails. Her thoughts were turning negative, so she increased the intensity of her run, making her too tired to think at all.

After three more miles, she made her way back to her grandparents' house. As she turned onto their street, she slowed to a walk so she could catch her breath before heading inside. Checking the time, she realized she had to hurry if she wanted to be ready by the time Abby was supposed to pick her up.

She quickly rid herself of her sweaty running clothes and hopped in the shower. They planned on going to lunch at their favorite diner, so Riley didn't feel any pressure to dress up. She put on jeans, a gray T-shirt, a maroon hoodie, and a pair of black Nikes. As she was tying the second shoe, she heard the doorbell ring, announcing Abby's arrival. She grabbed her wallet, phone, and keys and yelled out a goodbye to her parents and grandparents and opened the door for Abby.

Smiling, Abby said, "Hi. Were you running late? Your hair's still wet."

"Not really. I ran a little longer than I wanted, but I also didn't feel like drying my hair. Let's go."

As soon as they got in the car, Abby asked, "Is everything okay?"

Riley heard Abby's tone and figured Abby knew she had been running for a reason and had something on her mind.

"Yeah, I'm fine," Riley replied, looking out her window.

"If you want to talk about anything, I'm always here for you."

Riley gave her a brief smile. "I know, Abby, and I appreciate it. I don't really want to talk about it right now."

"Okay."

"So, where's Sara? I thought she would've come with you today."

"Oh, it's her mom's birthday. They have this whole mother-daughter birthday tradition. I'll go over there later tonight for dinner."

"That sounds fun. I'm glad I got to meet her last night. She seems really good for you, Abby."

Smiling broadly, Abby replied, "Thanks. She really is. Sometimes I can't even explain it. We both are super focused on school and have crazy goals we want to reach, but she still knows how to have fun. I feel pretty lucky that I met her."

Riley looked over at her ex-girlfriend and now friend, and she recognized the look on her face was the same look she got when she was thinking about Cam—dreamy, wistful, and deliriously happy. She was truly happy for Abby because she deserved the best.

They pulled into the diner's parking lot and could see Mike, Brian, and Katie waiting at a table for them. They used to frequent this diner at least once a week, so no one really needed to look at a menu anymore. As soon as the waitress came over, they all placed their orders. The guys started talking about a baseball tournament they had that coming weekend, and Katie and Abby discussed a history paper they had due the first week back from break. Everyone tried to bring Riley into the conversation, but she didn't give them much more than one-word answers, so they didn't try too hard for the rest of the meal.

After everyone had eaten and paid, they walked outside to say goodbye. Riley was only staying for one more day, so this was the last time she was going to see her friends. She gave everyone a hug and apologized for being quiet, which everyone shrugged off as no big deal. She shoved her hands into the pockets of her hoodie and walked back to the car with Abby.

She was startled out of her quiet contemplation when Abby said, "Let's go take a walk around the park."

"I've already done that today, several times, and at a quicker pace than a walk," Riley replied dryly.

"Well, humor me and take another lap at a leisurely pace."

"Fine."

They made the quick drive to the park and started their walk along the paved path circling the perimeter.

Almost five minutes passed in silence before Abby asked, "What's wrong? What happened?"

She let out a long, exasperated sigh. "I had a fight with Cam."

"About what?"

She opened her mouth to answer, but nothing came out.

"Riley, about what?"

She shoved her hands into the pocket of her hoodie. "You."

"What do you mean me?"

"I told her about hanging out with you last night and then again today and she got jealous."

Confused, Abby asked, "Didn't you tell her I have a girlfriend?"

She stopped in the middle of the path and raised her voice. "That shouldn't matter. She should trust me whether you're single or not."

"That's true but cut her some slack. She's having a pretty hard time at home."

Riley slumped her shoulders and stared at the ground as she shuffled her feet. "I know. I guess I just didn't expect it. And I'm sorry I snapped, Abby. You don't deserve that."

"Don't worry about it. I understand." Abby slipped her arm into Riley's and gently pulled her along.

"It's just super frustrating. I've never given her any reason not to trust me. I know she's totally thrown by the way Claire and her mom found out, and she's hurting more than she's willing to admit, but she shouldn't take it out on me."

"You know that's precisely who we always take out our problems on—the people that we love. I don't know why. Maybe we figure they'll always forgive us when we're being bitchy. I know I never hold it against you when you're being a bitch," she said with a smile and a nudge to Riley's shoulder.

"You're so funny." She tried to stay serious, but she couldn't stop the corners of her mouth from turning up slightly.

"Well, it's why we're friends," she replied with a smile before turning serious again. "Just give her some time. And when she comes around, make sure to talk with her about it. Don't hide how she's making you feel. She also deserves to know when things are bothering you."

"You're right. Don't worry, Abs. I don't want to mess this up. I'll talk to her."

"Good. Now let's get going. I need to change before I meet Sara at her house for dinner."

"Sounds good."

They walked back to the car in a silence that lasted the entire ride to Riley's grandparents' house. It was comfortable this time, not like the tension-filled silence of the ride to the park.

As Abby parked in the driveway, Riley turned and told her, "I'm really happy for you, Abby. Sara is great."

Smiling, Abby replied, "She is, and thank you. I'm happy for you too. I can tell how much Cam means to you. Don't let a little fight derail that."

"I won't." She leaned across the console and gave Abby a kiss on the cheek and held her tightly in a hug. "Bye, Abby."

"See ya, Riley."

She went into the house and up to her room to pack. She and her parents were leaving the next morning because her mom had a shift later that night. She didn't want to let this fight come between her and Cam, but she was hurt by the accusatory tone in Cam's voice. Maybe this time away from each other would be good for them. At least, maybe neither would say something they would regret or that would drive a bigger rift between them.

CHAPTER EIGHTEEN

Riley and Cam didn't talk on the phone for the rest of spring break. They shared a few texts every now and then, but the content of those never ventured past what they had done to occupy their days. Unfortunately, that made Cam even crankier than normal. Her first fight with Riley was a big one and fighting with her girlfriend sucked. Cam knew she had upset Riley and she couldn't believe she let her irritation with her dad fuel her jealousy. She was pissed at herself for her reaction and could only hope Riley would forgive her.

Most of the week with her dad had been filled with awkwardness, interspersed with some periods of fun. They had a good time at the zoo and one day, they went across the river into Newport to visit the aquarium. While they both had a great time, they still didn't talk about anything besides the usual things like sports, school, and college. It seemed her dad was giving her the space she asked for and was just waiting for her to open up.

Cam's last day in Cincinnati was a Sunday, so before going back to Indy, they stopped for brunch at a diner down the street from her dad's house. She understood why he loved this place as soon as she tasted the food. It was probably the best French toast she had ever had, and she ate it quickly, barely stopping to breathe. She was grateful for the high quality of the food as well as the amount, because her appetite had been close to nonexistent lately. She finished her last bite and raised her head to see her dad looking at her with amusement.

"Hungry, were you?" Cam simply nodded as a look of concern washed over his face. "How about we pay and then go sit on a bench in the park across the street?"

"Sure."

They walked out to enjoy the bright sunshine and welcoming warm temperature. They found an empty bench after a brief walk along the trail that intersected the park. Her dad stretched out his legs and crossed them at the ankles, resting his arms along the back of the bench. Cam sat about a foot away from him, her hands at her sides. She leaned forward to watch kids playing on the playground and runners and walkers passing by them on the trail.

Eventually her dad broke his silence. "Cam, I'm sorry."

She heard the pain in his voice and saw the sincerity in his eyes.

"I know this week hasn't been the best. Did you have any fun?"

"Of course, Dad," she said with a small smile.

"Look, I'm not trying to push you to talk. I know you've had a difficult time, especially with Mom and Claire. I'm really sorry I've added to your stress. Your mom and I love you so much. Yes, this has all been a surprise, but I think you've been misunderstanding us as much as we have you."

She looked at him with a questioning gaze.

"This push-back you've been getting from us hasn't been because we're disappointed in you. We aren't and we never could be. We're just scared, Cam."

"Scared? What do you mean?"

He let out a heavy sigh and said, "Sweetie, I know you've probably figured this out a little bit, but the world can be a mean and hateful place. We don't want to see you discriminated against, ridiculed, or even physically hurt because of who you love. We're scared of that, and we know there will be times we won't be able to stop it. That's an awful feeling for a parent to have. Being a cop, I've unfortunately had the opportunity to see the worst of humanity. I'm not trying to scare you, but hate crimes are very real. Your safety is of the utmost importance to me. Just thinking about anything happening to you is like a punch to the gut. Even though you're growing into a beautiful young woman, you will always be our little girl. Your mom and I will never stop trying to protect you from any bad thing that might come your way. I hope you know that."

Cam started to cry, and she turned away before her dad could see. But she knew she wasn't hiding it well because she was fighting to get a full breath as she tried to hold back the sobs. As soon as he rubbed her back and said comforting words, she wrapped her arms around him tightly. He hugged and comforted her like he used to when she was a kid and she'd hurt herself. After a few moments, she pulled back to wipe her eyes.

"Sorry, Dad. I got your shirt all wet."

"Don't worry. It'll dry. I want you to understand how much I love you."

Smiling, she said, "I love you too, Dad."

He squeezed her hand and said, "Well, we should get going. Don't want to get you home too late since you have school in the morning."

They got up and started walking toward the parking lot.

He stopped when Cam said, "Thanks, Dad."

Smiling, he reached out his arm and pulled her into an embrace.

The ride home was quiet, but it was a thousand times more comfortable than the drive to Cincinnati. They didn't talk much, but they did enjoy two hours of singing along to the radio. They were always able to bond over their love of music. He always told her that playing music when she was fussy as a baby was the only way he could soothe her. Her mom was always able to rock her to quiet her, but her dad would quietly sing his favorite songs to her. Today in the car, he even tried to rap along to some of the songs when it was Cam's turn to pick the radio station, not caring that he was making a fool of himself.

He pulled into the driveway and shut off the car. Before opening his door, he turned to Cam and said, "I'm glad we got to spend some one-on-one time this week, Cam. I know we don't get to do that enough, and I'm sorry for that. I just want you to know that you can always talk to me about anything. And, if you ever need me to come home, tell me, and I will get here as soon as I can." He reached over and squeezed her hand.

"Thanks, Dad. I really appreciate that."

"Okay, ready to go in?"

"Um, sure," Cam said hesitantly.

He carried her bag inside and Cam heard her mom coming down the stairs.

"Cameron!" She wrapped Cam in a surprisingly tight hug. Her mom whispered in her ear, "I missed you, sweetie."

At first, she tensed, but she quickly disregarded the problems between them and returned the hug with an equal amount of strength. "I missed you too, Mom."

And, that was true. Cam hated the rift that had come between them. Sure, she wouldn't tell her mom everything like Riley did with hers, but she missed all the time she used to spend with her mom and brothers. She knew they were both to blame for the fight, but she really didn't know how to fix things when her mom still had a hard time looking at her, let alone talking with her.

Her mom held her by her shoulders. "Did you have a good time?"

Cam looked at her dad with a knowing smile, and replied, "Yeah, I did. I'm gonna take my stuff upstairs." She gave her father a strong hug. "Bye, Dad. Thanks for everything."

"You're welcome, sweetheart."

She headed upstairs, but she stopped when she heard her mom ask, "So, how did it really go?"

He let out a small sigh, and replied, "Well, you know from our phone call how that first night went. Things were tense throughout the week, but we had a really good talk this morning after breakfast. I think we understand each other better. I told her that we're just scared for her, and I think she saw where I was coming from."

"What do you think we should do? I mean, do you think this is serious with Riley?"

"I really think it is. Her face lights up like you wouldn't believe when she talks about her."

"Oh, I know. I noticed it before everything blew up, but I thought it was just because they were becoming really good friends." Her mom let out a chuckle. "I didn't expect them to become *that* good of friends."

Cam sat on the top step and peered down at the scene below. She didn't know that she had been that obvious when it came to talking about Riley. Her emotions were still raw. Hearing her dad stand up for her choked her up, but she was still wary about what her mom thought about everything.

"You should talk to her sometime, T. I mean, really talk to her. She's a great kid. You've done an amazing job with her."

"Thanks, Tony."

Cam looked down at her parents with a sense of longing for the past, when they were together and happy. She knew things had improved since her father moved, but she still held on to the childlike hope that her parents would get back together. Seeing them like they were now only reinforced that feeling. Her dad placed a quick kiss on her mom's cheek and he said, "I'll talk to you later."

Her mom nodded silently and closed the door. She pressed her forehead against it, and Cam, suddenly feeling like an intruder, turned away.

CHAPTER NINETEEN

The first day of school after break was the first time Cam had seen Riley since their fight, and she couldn't shake the nerves she'd had since waking up. Throughout the day, they both seemed unsure how to approach each other, even though they had a couple classes together. So saying hi was the extent of their conversation during school.

As the day came to an end, Cam couldn't take the silence anymore. Before she changed her mind, she headed toward Riley's locker, hoping to catch her before she left. As Cam turned the corner into the senior hallway, she exhaled as she saw Riley exchanging her books. She walked up behind her and gently cleared her throat. "Riley?"

Riley turned around and looked at Cam. "Oh, hey."

Cam tried not to wince at the hesitancy and sadness radiating from Riley's body language and eyes. "Hey," Cam replied quietly. Biting her lower lip, she dropped her gaze to the ground. "C-can we talk, please?" She waited several seconds, but finally looked up because Riley was taking too long to answer.

Riley took a deep breath and let it out slowly. "Sure." She closed her locker, picked up her bag, and led Cam down a side hallway. She dropped her backpack on the floor and crossed her arms.

Cam wrung her hands together as she paced back and forth, but it was becoming obvious that Riley was waiting for her talk. It was hard for her to look Riley in the eye because she couldn't stand to see the pain in them—the pain she had caused.

"I'm so, so sorry, Riley. I was an idiot. I had no right to be jealous of you and Abby hanging out. You're allowed to hang out with anyone you want. I know you would never do anything to deliberately hurt me. It's not an excuse, but I was just in a shitty mood because of the talk with my dad and feeling like my mom just passed me off to him. And I took it out on you. I'm sorry." Cam stopped in front of Riley and as a tear made its way down her cheek, she took a deep breath and met her gaze. "I trust you with all that I am, Riley. Please, please forgive me. I love you."

Riley moved closer and cradled Cam's face in her hands. She brushed a few of Cam's tears away. As she started talking, her eyes also filled with tears.

"You're right. There was no reason for you to be jealous. I was up front about what I was doing and who I was hanging out with. I know things have been rough, but I am not your punching bag. We need to be able to trust each other if we want this to work." She closed her eyes briefly and a few tears spilled out. Cam brushed them away with her thumb and Riley leaned into her touch. Riley took a deep breath and opened her eyes. She whispered, "And I love you too, Cameron."

Riley kissed the tears from each cheek before tentatively brushing her lips against Cam's. They both let out a sigh of relief before Riley kissed Cam more deliberately. Before they got too caught up in the moment, they wrapped their arms around each other tightly. Cam breathed in deeply as she nuzzled Riley's neck, and she was comforted by her familiar scent. Cam lost track of how long they stood like that, but she felt a sense of peace as the time passed. They pulled away from each other with huge grins on their faces as they picked up their backpacks and walked side by side out of the school.

Riley stopped when they reached Cam's car. There were still some people lingering in the parking lot, so Riley lightly grasped Cam's pinky finger with hers. "I'll talk to you later, okay?"

"Okay. I love you."

"I love you too. Have a good night, Cam." She squeezed Cam's pinky one last time before heading toward her own car.

* * *

As soon as Cam walked into school the next day, she instantly knew something was wrong. Most of the seniors gave her strange looks and their conversations seemed to stop as she made her way down the hallway. It made her nervous, and her eyes darted back and forth to classmates lingering in the hallway.

Walking up to Riley's locker, Cam asked, "Is something going on? Does it seem like everyone is staring at me?"

Riley had a troubled, fearful look in her eyes as she looked around quickly. Then she whispered, "Meet me in the bathroom in the science hallway fifteen minutes after our first class starts." Cam was about to say something, but Riley interrupted, "Please, Cam?"

Mutely, Cam nodded as Riley picked up her backpack and walked down the hallway to her first class. Cam tried to choke down the rising panic as she focused on collecting the books she needed for the first half of the day. She couldn't stop her trembling hands as she closed her locker and walked to class.

While she sat in her first class, the minutes seemed to go by at a snail's pace. As soon as fifteen minutes had passed, her hand shot in the air and she asked the teacher to use the bathroom. Cam hurried toward the designated bathroom without attracting any attention from the few teachers and students she passed in the halls. Once she was in the bathroom, Riley quickly closed the door and locked it behind her.

"What the hell is going on, Riley?"

With a slight hint of fear in her voice, she replied, "I think someone saw us yesterday after school."

Cam covered her mouth with her hand as she whispered, "How do you know?"

Riley averted her gaze. "That's not important. But if—"

"How, Riley?"

"I found a note in my locker. It's not a big deal."

"What did it say?"

"It's not important, Cam."

"Tell me," Cam replied even louder.

Sighing, she looked at the ground and said quietly, "It just said, 'We don't want you here dyke—go back to Illinois.'"

Closing her eyes, Cam took a deep breath and wrapped Riley in a tight hug. "I'm so sorry, Riley," she whispered as she lightly pressed her lips to Riley's neck.

"You're sorry? Cam, I'm sorry for you. I know how private you are and how you don't like any unwanted attention." Reluctantly, she broke away from Cam's embrace as she continued in a pained voice. "I'll understand if you want to distance yourself from me, especially while we're at school. But please don't tell me I'll lose you completely."

"Whoa, whoa," Cam replied quickly as she grasped Riley's hands in hers. "I'm not letting that happen. If people want to think we're together, whatever. My family and Claire already know about us, and they were the only ones I was scared to tell. I'll be honest, though. I'm not going to offer up any information to anyone, but I can't help what others think. We'll just have to ignore it all. Okay?"

Riley faintly nodded but her eyes were locked on the ground. Cam placed two fingers underneath her chin, lifted her face, and gently kissed her. She looked Riley in the eyes and whispered, "I love you. This doesn't change anything."

"I love you too." Straightening, Riley said, "We should get back to class. You go first. I'll leave in a couple minutes."

"Okay." Cam gave a final squeeze as she said, "I'll see you later." She walked back to class in a slight daze. *Well so much for being just another face in the crowd.*

Knowing why she was being stared at earlier in the day made Cam feel slightly less self-conscious. She tried to ignore the looks and the whispers, but she couldn't shut them all out.

She knew it was inevitable that someone would find out about her and Riley. She had just hoped it would've been closer to the end of the school year. Aside from one or two whispered slurs as she walked in the crowded hallways between classes, she mostly got curious stares throughout the day. She wasn't so naïve to think she would never face any hatred or discrimination for being with another girl, but it was still painful to hear, especially from kids in her own school. As she reached her locker after the last bell, she took a deep breath, relieved the day was over.

She closed her locker and was surprised to see Bri standing a few feet away, seemingly waiting for her.

"Hey, Cam."

"Hi," Cam replied, hesitant and unsure of what Bri was about to say.

"I've heard the talk going around school. I'm sorry people are being jerks. I've heard the rumors about me before so I know a little of what you're feeling. So if you need someone to vent to, let me know."

"Wow, thanks. That means a lot."

"No problem. I should get going." She took a step back and stopped, saying with a big smile. "Oh, and you and Riley are really cute together."

Blushing, Cam replied, "Thanks. I'm sorry you guys didn't work."

She waved her off. "Nah, no big deal. She's a good friend. See ya."

Cam turned and walked down the hallway toward the exit when she heard loud voices coming from a side hallway. She came upon Claire yelling at Jenny and Britt—the two "mean girls" on the soccer team and the only ones Claire, Riley, and Cam had tried to distance themselves from during the season.

"Grow the fuck up, Jenny. Cam and Riley don't deserve you spreading rumors around about them."

Jenny fired back, "But we had to change in front of them. We should have known that they were dykes."

As soon as that was out of Jenny's mouth, Claire closed the distance until her face was only an inch away from Jenny's and she pressed two fingers against Jenny's sternum. "Shut your mouth. If I hear you or anyone else say something bad about Cam, you will regret it. Don't think I won't hurt you, because I will. Got it?"

With anger in her eyes, Jenny nodded, and she pushed Claire out of the way. Then she and Britt left in the opposite direction. Cam didn't want Claire to know she had overheard everything, but it was as if her feet were glued to the floor as she stared at Claire. Claire leaned her forehead against the wall and took several slow breaths.

As if she sensed she was being watched, Claire turned in Cam's direction and was obviously startled to find her standing there. They both stared at each other in shock, mouths open and eyes wide. Finally, Claire slung her backpack over her shoulder and walked toward Cam on her way out of the building.

Cam lightly grasped her arm and looked into her eyes until she finally found enough strength to whisper, "Thanks."

Cam thought she saw tears in Claire's eyes, but Claire nodded imperceptibly as she moved out of Cam's grasp and continued down the hallway. Finally, she had a sliver of hope to hold on to that she and Claire would work everything out.

When Cam got home that night after a short shift at the library, she found her mom in the kitchen putting a salad together for dinner. Even though her mom barely worked at the restaurant anymore, it still felt weird to come home and find her there, especially on a weeknight. She seemed less stressed in general, and she was able to spend more time with the boys and had even started going out with her friends again.

After today, Cam understood her parents' fear after hearing some of the hateful comments from her fellow classmates. As her mom chopped cucumbers and tomatoes for the salad, she debated whether to tell her mom what happened at school. She didn't want to add any more stress to her plate, but she also thought talking about it might help open the lines of communication between them.

"Hey, Mom. What's for dinner?"

"Oh, hey there. We're having lasagna and salad. That sound good?"

"Sounds delicious." Cam and her mom awkwardly looked at each other for a moment before Cam took a seat at the kitchen table.

"How was your day?"

"Well, it wasn't the best, but it wasn't awful either."

Her mom wiped her hands on a kitchen towel before taking a seat next to Cam. "Did something happen?"

Cam hesitated but decided she should try and be honest with her. "Not really. But, um, people found out that Riley and I are together."

Her mom flinched as if she had been slapped. "Are you okay? Did anyone say anything?"

"I'm…I'm okay." She could tell her mom was struggling with this information and she didn't want to make anything worse, so she held back a bit of the truth. Her mom wasn't the only one who wanted to shield others from pain. "People were okay. I got a few more stares throughout the day, but it wasn't too bad."

"That's good." Cam could tell her mom didn't believe her. "I'm sorry things have been difficult for you, Cam. And I know I haven't reacted the way you hoped. All I ask is that you be patient with me—that we be patient with each other. Think you can do that?"

"Sure."

"Can you go tell your brothers it's time for dinner?"

"Will do."

Just before she hit the stairs, her mom called out, "I love you, Cam. I hope you know that."

"I know. I love you too, Mom." Her mom nodded and turned back to the salad.

While it wasn't a warm and fuzzy moment, she was happy that it seemed like she had made a tiny bit of progress. *Maybe dinners won't be as awkward anymore. One can hope, right?*

Later that night as Cam sat on her bed finishing up her homework, she heard a soft knock on the door.

"Come in."

The door opened but Cam wanted to finish one last question. After writing her answer down, she looked up, her eyes widening in complete surprise. "Claire."

Claire looked extremely uncomfortable as she stood in the doorway and dug her toes into the carpet. "Um, hey. Can I come in?"

"Y-yeah," Cam replied as she gathered her books and papers spread across her bed. She placed the pile on the floor and sat back against the headboard, hugging her knees to her chest.

Claire closed the door softly before placing her purse on Cam's desk.

"Can I sit down?"

"Oh yeah. Of course," Cam replied quickly.

Claire gingerly sat near the foot of the bed, looking anxious as she wrung her hands together in her lap. They sat there in silence for several moments, neither making eye contact with the other.

"I'm sorry," they said in unison. Looking at each other, they burst out laughing.

They wiped away the tears that were either from laughing or crying, Cam wasn't sure, but they eventually composed themselves.

Taking a deep breath, Cam said, "Claire, I'm so sorry I kept things from you. I just had a hard time processing it all. I didn't want to push you away or freak you out. Then when things with Riley started…I don't know." She looked down and shook her head. "I didn't want to risk anything, risk losing her," she said with a shrug and met Claire's gaze again.

"I get that. But I'm not gonna lie; it really hurt, Cameron." Claire looked away briefly and cleared her throat before continuing. "So, um, you're a lesbian now? Was everything with Danny fake?"

"No, not at all. I did love him, but at some point, I realized it was love for a friend and nothing more. And I identify as bi. If I'm going to be honest with myself, there's always been girls that I thought were cute or felt drawn to, but I thought it just meant that I wanted to be like them instead of wanting to be *with* them. And since I'm attracted to guys too, I thought that was enough and what I should do. I didn't want to be different, and people's expectations were for me to find a boyfriend. But when Riley came along, I don't know…I just couldn't help myself."

"I get that. I really do. And I don't even care about you being bi. Me getting upset never had anything to do with your sexuality and it's not going to change anything between us. It just hurt so much that you hid it from me. You're my best friend, practically my sister. I will always love and support you. You need to talk to me. I feel like you've been lying to me for months, maybe even years. How could you do that? I don't know what's going on with you and Riley, but—"

"I'm in love with her."

"You're what?"

"I'm in love with her," she whispered as she stared at the floor, thinking Claire was mad at her for that confession. Before she could look up, Claire moved forward and wrapped her arms around Cam.

"I do want you to be happy. I hope you know that."

Cam hugged Claire tighter and buried her face in Claire's neck. "Thanks. I'm so sorry I lied and hid everything from you. I promise not to do that ever again." She pulled away to look in Claire's eyes. "Are we okay?"

"Definitely. I should probably apologize too. I feel like I should have seen something. Like I said, you're my best friend. I think as time went on I got more and more embarrassed that I had no idea about any of this, never even had an inkling. How did I miss this?"

"It's fine, Claire. I didn't give you much to work with. We both know I don't talk much about myself."

"Yeah, no shit," Claire responded with a laugh. "I do understand why you thought you needed to hide it. I'm not trying to belittle you at all. It's a big and scary realization. But I still need to apologize. I've been so wrapped up in Luke since we started dating. I know I haven't been as available to hang out and chat like I have been in the past. And that's all on me. I should have realized I was spending so much time with him that it was hurting our friendship. Can you forgive me?"

"Of course. It's all over and done with. Time to move on, okay?"

Claire grabbed her by the shoulders and pulled her in for another hug. "Okay," she whispered against Cam's neck.

Cam sat back and brushed a lingering tear off her cheek. She cleared her throat and said, "I also need to thank you. It meant a lot to see you stand up for me and Riley."

"I will always stand up for you, Cam. Jenny and Britt are bitches, plain and simple. There is nothing wrong with you or Riley. You got that?" Cam nodded. "You deserve love and happiness, and I will not let anyone get in your way of finding that."

"Thanks."

"Now, you need to tell me everything," Claire said with a grin.

Cam let out a deep breath, and began. "Well, I first saw her at the library this summer…"

CHAPTER TWENTY

By the end of the week, everyone seemed to have forgotten that Riley and Cam were together. They still received a few curious looks every now and then, but none of the looks held animosity behind them. Riley didn't know if it was because everyone accepted them as a couple or if they had just moved on to the newer gossip about a football player getting caught selling pot. Either way, Riley was happy that things had returned to relative normalcy. Not happy the guy got in trouble. Just happy the spotlight wasn't on her or Cam anymore.

"Hey, there," Cam said as Riley was texting her from the parking lot.

"Hey," Riley replied in surprise. "I thought you had a meeting."

"I was supposed to, but I stopped by Mrs. Quinn's room to talk about the paper, but she had to pick up her kids, so she asked to reschedule."

"That sucks. Do you need any help with it?"

"No, I should be okay. It's not due for another couple weeks."

Riley nodded and said, "We should get going. You have to work."

Instead of answering, Cam sweetly kissed her. "Would you like to get dinner tonight?"

Riley furrowed her brows in confusion. "I thought you had to work tonight."

"I do, but they said they only needed me for about two to three hours, so I should be done by six-ish."

"What about your mom? I don't want you to get into any trouble."

Shrugging, Cam replied, "She won't know. I didn't tell her they shortened my shift, so she still thinks it ends at eight."

Still concerned, Riley asked, "Are you sure?"

"Positive. Plus, I told her I would probably just spend the night at Claire's, so I thought…"

Riley realized what Cam was hinting at and she cracked a grin. "Would you like to spend the night?"

Cam gave her a wink. "Well, that's a great idea. Why didn't I think of that? And yes. Yes, I would." She took Riley's hand in hers and said, "Let me walk you to your car."

As they walked through the parking lot, Riley thought about how far Cam had come with her comfort level about publicly showing affection since they were outed at the beginning of the week. Sure, it helped that most of the students and teachers had quickly left once the bell rang since it was Friday, but Riley cherished these little victories in the progress of Cam's comfort with their relationship.

Suddenly Claire appeared, heading toward them. Riley started to pull her hand away from Cam, but Cam gripped it tighter.

"Hey, guys," Claire said hesitantly.

Cam replied with a cheerful greeting, while Riley's more closely mirrored Claire's. Cam had filled Riley in on her reconciliation with Claire, but Riley had yet to talk to Claire since she caught them that fateful day in Cam's bedroom.

"Can I talk to you for a minute, Riley?"

"Sure," Riley replied as she gave Cam a brief glance, one that was full of uncertainty. Cam quietly stepped back a few feet to give them privacy.

Riley nervously toyed with her necklace as Claire stepped closer.

"I'm sorry, Riley. I never gave either of you a chance to explain everything that was going on. I'm really sorry I shut you out all this time. I hope you can forgive me."

"Of course," Riley replied as she let go of the breath she had been holding. "I should have reached out to you after the fact too. I just didn't want to get between you two," she said with a slight nod toward Cam. "You're like a sister to her, ya know?"

Claire nodded solemnly. "I know. I feel the same way about her." She gave Riley a hug and whispered in her ear, "She deserves all the happiness in the world. And, while I like you and you're a great friend—you hurt her, I hurt you." Claire pulled back and cupped Riley's face in her hands. "Got it?"

"I got it," Riley replied, trying not to smile. She wanted Claire to think she had scared her at least a little.

"Good. I have to head home to have dinner with my family. You're spending the night, right Cam?" She emphasized the question with an over-exaggerated wink.

Laughing, Cam stepped closer to the duo and replied, "I am. So nice of you to let me stay over."

Claire let out a loud chuckle. "Right. I'll see you guys later," she said as she walked away.

"I can't help but notice that you seem to be at ease with people seeing us together. How are you okay with all this?"

Cam shrugged. "I don't know." She took a deep breath and wrapped her arms around Riley's waist. "All I know is that I love you, Riley, and I'm not going to let anyone push you away. I've also realized that I can be protective of those I love when someone or something is threatening them. Now that people know, I don't want to hide. You're my girlfriend and I'm not ashamed of that. I'm still nervous about whether my mom will ever fully come around, but I'm okay with people seeing us as long as you are."

"I'm definitely okay with it, Cam. I'm not gonna lie. It's going to be nice to openly date you now. I can take you out, hold your hand, and show you off if I want to."

"I'll pick you up at six thirty, okay?"

"Sounds good," Riley replied as she drew her closer for a kiss.

"I'll see you later."

Unable to resist, Riley gave Cam a final quick kiss and headed home to wait for their date.

As soon as her shift ended, Cam drove over to Riley's house. Before she got a chance to knock on the door, Riley opened it and pulled Cam inside for a heated kiss. Cam let out a surprised whimper, dropped her backpack to the floor, and wrapped her arms tightly around Riley's neck before deepening the kiss even further.

Needing to catch her breath, Cam pulled back with a lopsided grin on her face. "Well, that's a wonderful welcome."

"Sorry. I didn't mean to attack you like that," Riley said as she shuffled her feet and averted her gaze.

"Riley, you can greet me like that anytime to you want. You'll get no complaints from me. Wait, your parents aren't home, are they?" Cam asked, panicked.

"No, they had some charity event to go to. My mom said they won't be home until midnight."

"Oh really?" Cam asked as she wiggled her eyebrows suggestively.

"Really," Riley replied as she leaned in for another lingering kiss.

Cam hesitantly asked, "Can we go up to your room?"

Knowing the implication of that question, Riley's eyes widened slightly. "Are you sure? What about dinner?"

Cam smiled as she stared at Riley's lips and replied in a husky voice, "Dinner can wait. I don't want to anymore."

She grabbed her by the hand and led Riley upstairs to her room. Once they got inside, Cam walked toward the end of the bed and Riley locked the door. As Riley turned toward the bed, Cam clenched her fists as her confidence faded.

Riley seemed to sense Cam's hesitation. She grabbed Cam's hands and placed soft kisses on her knuckles. "We don't have to do anything, Cam. There's no rush."

Squeezing her hands gently, Cam gazed at Riley and whispered, "I want this, Riley. I want you."

Cam kissed her softly, hesitantly. But with the first swipe of Riley's tongue against her lower lip, she responded with a hunger that had been building for months. She buried her hands in Riley's hair. They were so close that a breath of wind couldn't pass between them. Cam's knees hit the end of the bed and she lowered herself to sit. They broke apart as Cam scooted back to lie on the bed and Riley hovered over her.

Cam pulled Riley down for another kiss. Even those few seconds apart made her miss the warmth and pressure of Riley's lips. Riley slipped her leg between Cam's thighs, causing the pulse between Cam's legs to increase tenfold. She gasped into Riley's mouth. As Riley ground into Cam, she slowly moved her hand to the bottom of Cam's T-shirt. Her fingertips lightly brushed Cam's side and she shivered despite her heat. She sat up once Riley pushed her shirt higher, allowing her to remove it before lowering herself to the bed again and bringing Riley with her.

She rubbed her hands down Riley's back, grabbing her shirt and pulling it over her head. Riley sat back on her heels and Cam slowly brushed her hand down Riley's chest between her breasts and down her stomach until she rested her hand on Riley's hip, caressing the skin with her thumb. Cam was starting to feel almost dizzy with excitement.

"Jesus, Riley. You're just...wow."

Riley smiled shyly. "I could say the same about you."

Cam tightened her grip, sitting up to pull Riley in for a fiery kiss. Riley cupped Cam's cheek, holding her tightly as she pushed Cam's upper body back down to the bed. Riley reached behind Cam and quickly discarded her bra. She trailed kisses down the side of Cam's neck until her hands rested at the button of Cam's jeans.

Riley looked up to meet Cam's gaze. "You okay? We can stop."

"Please, Riley. Keep going." Cam didn't know her voice could sound so desperate, but she couldn't help wanting more of Riley and she wasn't going to stop until she had all of her.

Quickly, they stripped off their remaining clothes, and Riley settled back on top of Cam, both groaning at the complete skin-to-skin contact. Riley pressed kisses along the length of Cam's neck and shoulders as her hands slowly moved lower. She trailed her fingers on the outside of Cam's thigh, circling her knee and gently pushing her legs open. Riley watched Cam's reaction as she moved her hand between her legs and slowly entered her. Cam arched into her touch, letting out a sharp gasp. With each stroke, Riley went deeper and faster, and Cam's breathing quickened until she threw her head back against the pillow as she came, gripping Riley's forearm so tightly that Riley worried she might leave bruises.

As Cam controlled her breathing and slowly relaxed, Riley gently brushed soft kisses across her shoulder, neck, and cheek until she finally reached Cam's lips for a languid, tender kiss.

"Are you okay?"

Stroking Riley's cheek with her thumb, Cam replied softly, "Oh yeah. Much better than okay."

Riley let out a relieved breath. Cam kissed her hungrily. She didn't have the words to describe how wonderful Riley had just made her feel, so she tried to convey her feelings through her actions.

Grabbing Riley's hips, she rolled Riley over. Cam pressed between Riley's legs and leaned down to capture Riley's lips with hers. Now that Cam had Riley's beautiful, naked body beneath her, she studied her tattoo, finally seeing the entire art for the first time. Cam lightly traced the feather and birds with her fingers until she brushed delicate kisses along its length. Riley shuddered, let out a groan, and moved her fingers into Cam's hair.

Cam lifted her head and looked into Riley's eyes with passion and a hint of hesitation as she said, "I may need your help."

Riley seemed to understand Cam's request and she placed her hand on top of hers and moved it to where she needed it most. Once Cam had found a rhythm, Riley let her hand fall to the side and she gripped the sheets.

With renewed confidence, Cam's hands and mouth seemed to move as if by instinct. Within minutes, Riley grasped the back of Cam's neck so their foreheads were touching. She looked into Cam's eyes and let out a strangled whisper. "Right there. Almost…"

Cam kissed Riley just as she let out a low moan and slowed her strokes to bring Riley down from that incredible high. Cam didn't know if she had ever seen a more beautiful sight. She collapsed on top of Riley and placed a soft kiss on the underside of Riley's jaw. Riley still pulsed beneath her hand, lying there, utterly spent. It hadn't been her intention to sleep with Riley when they made plans for their date. But now that she had, she couldn't imagine wanting to be anywhere other than in Riley's arms and feeling the warmth of her skin pressed against hers.

They rested in comfortable, sated silence. Riley sat up, dislodging Cam to grab the sheet. She wrapped Cam in her arms and pulled the sheet over their bodies. Tightening her arm around Cam, Riley kissed her bare shoulder and whispered into her ear, "God, this feels so good." Cam settled against Riley and hummed in affirmation. They stayed like that until Cam's stomach growled.

"Someone hungry?" Riley asked with amusement.

"Maybe."

"How about we order a pizza?"

"Sounds good."

Riley got out of bed and put on a long-sleeve shirt and pair of shorts, but Cam just sat up and shyly held the sheet against her chest. "Um, can I borrow a T-shirt and shorts?"

"Sure. But ya know, you can stay like that all night long. Might be a hardship, but I think I can take it," she said as she tossed the clothes to Cam.

Cam's cheeks reddened and she hummed in reply. She got dressed with her back to Riley, still feeling shy despite what they had just done.

Before they could walk out of the room, Riley stopped Cam with a hand on her hip. "Are you okay…" Riley flicked her eyes to the disheveled bed and back to Cam, "…with everything?"

A slow smile spread across Cam's face. "Oh yeah."

Riley smiled as she let out a breath. "Good. Me too."

After ordering the pizza, they sat on the couch to start a movie while they waited for it to arrive. They spent the rest of the evening munching on the pizza, cuddled together on the couch.

Riley cleared her throat. "So, I've started getting acceptance letters for college."

Over the course of the fall semester, Riley, Cam, and Claire had helped each other with applications. They proofread essays, narrowed down schools to limit the amount of application fees they had to pay, and acted as moral support when needed. They had talked in generalities about how awesome it would be for all of them to go the same school, but deep down they knew that was never going to happen, especially when their interests were so vastly different. Once Riley and Cam had sent in all their applications, they had agreed to see which schools they got into before discussing their options. Neither one wanted to think about the possibility of not choosing the same school so they decided to postpone talking about anything related to college until they started getting acceptance letters and their decisions about where to go became unavoidable.

"Me too," Cam replied as she gripped Riley's fingers.

"What do you think you're gonna do?"

"I don't know. I need to stay in state. I can't really afford not to."

"I know," Riley replied.

"I'm still undecided on my major but I think I'm leaning toward English. And Purdue has a really good program. Plus, I'd be close enough to come back whenever I needed or wanted to see my mom or brothers. What do you think?"

"I think that sounds like a pretty great plan."

Cam heard the sincerity in her words, but she also saw the sadness in Riley's eyes. "You've decided where you're going, haven't you?"

Riley nodded. "I'm going back to Champaign, to go to Illinois. Their computer science program is one of the best."

"Right," Cam whispered as she averted her gaze.

Riley lifted her chin and rubbed her thumb along Cam's bottom lip. "We're going to be okay, Cam," she said, pressing a soft kiss to Cam's lips.

"How can you be so sure?" Cam asked as her voice cracked.

"Because it's us. My parents will be here, so this is where I'll always come for breaks. We can text, talk, video chat, write letters, whatever. I want this to work. Sure, it's gonna suck, but we're going to be fine. Okay?"

"Okay."

They returned their attention to the movie, holding each other a little tighter than before. Riley had to nudge Cam awake as the credits rolled.

"Is it over?"

"Yeah. Let's head up to bed."

Cam sleepily nodded and followed Riley up the stairs. After brushing their teeth, they went into the bedroom and Riley closed her door. They each got into the bed on their typical side and rolled over to face each other.

"Goodnight, Cam," Riley said.

With the first touch of Riley's goodnight kiss, Cam was no longer tired. She slowly deepened the kiss, gently brushing her tongue against Riley's bottom lip. Cam slid her fingers under Riley's shirt and she broke the kiss to help Riley take it off. Cam said, "Oh, I don't plan on going to sleep just yet."

She pressed her hand to Riley's chest and rolled over until she covered Riley. She placed an open-mouth kiss to the base of Riley's throat and drew a path down her chest as she let herself get lost in the wonder of Riley's body.

CHAPTER TWENTY-ONE

Finals week flew by and Cam thought she did well considering all the distractions she had recently. She finished her finals by Wednesday and she was happy to have a couple of days to herself while her mom and brothers still had school. She was able to relax and reflect on all the events, good and bad, that had taken place during her last year of high school. It was surreal for her to think about how she would be moving out on her own in a couple months. Fighting with her mom had made her feel slightly isolated at home, and she was looking forward to the day when she would be on her own and able to live her life the way she wanted.

That Friday, Cam's dad arrived for graduation weekend—just as pizza was being delivered. As soon as he paid, he took the pizza into the kitchen and everyone filled their plates before sitting down to eat. Conversation throughout the meal was easy, and Cam loved seeing the joy on her brothers' faces as they talked with their dad, catching them up on the last few days of school and how they were doing on their baseball teams.

Her mom also seemed to be in better spirits throughout the meal. Once they had finished, her dad suggested they spend the evening playing a few board games. Cam found herself enjoying the talk and laughter that went on throughout the night.

While the evening had gone smoothly, Cam just wanted to relax and have some quiet time to herself, so she decided to head up to her room and read. She had been reading for over an hour, reclining on her bed, propped up by a few pillows, when she heard a soft knock on her half-open door. She looked up to see her mom standing in the doorway, looking hesitant.

"Hey, Cam. Mind if I come in?"

"Sure, Mom."

Cam closed her book and placed it on her nightstand. She pulled her legs up and wrapped her arms around them, hugging them to her chest. Her mom sat on the bed a few inches away, rubbing the back of her neck with her hand, which was a sure sign that she was uncomfortable.

"What's up?"

She met Cam's gaze and placed her hand on the outside of Cam's ankle, softly rubbing circles with her thumb. "Cameron, I need to apologize to you. I know I hurt you terribly by saying those things when I found out about you and Riley. I'm not saying I completely understand your sexuality, but I'm willing to learn. I don't want this to push you away, especially with you moving out soon. I know the past couple of years have been hard on you, with your dad and me fighting and then the divorce. I know I put a lot of responsibility on your shoulders with Josh and Ethan."

"It's okay, Mom."

"No, it's not, sweetie." She grabbed a tissue off Cam's desk to dab at her tears. "I can't believe you're heading to college in a couple months. I don't want you to leave with any hesitation about how much I love you. I just want you to know how proud I am of you. You have grown into a beautiful, smart, and caring young woman. I am incredibly proud and grateful to be your mother. All I want is for you to be happy. You shouldn't have to hide who you are, especially among your family. You're incredibly brave for figuring out who you are at this age and standing by it. I will always be by your side to support you. I hope you know that."

As tears fell down her cheeks, she wrapped her arms around her mom. "I do know that. I love you."

"I love you too, Cameron."

They sat there hugging until their tears had stopped.

Cam knew this had been a major turning point for them. Throughout her mother's apology, she never doubted the sincerity in her voice. While she had been deeply hurt by her mom's reaction, she wanted to put it all behind her and regain the relationship they had before everything happened, and hopefully improve upon it as well.

"So, are things going okay with Riley?" her mom asked hesitantly.

Smiling wide, Cam replied, "Yeah, they are."

"I'm sorry I stopped letting you see her. I just didn't know how to handle it."

"Mom, stop. You've apologized. We can't change what happened. Let's just move on."

Her mom nodded as she gently squeezed Cam's hand. "So, you like her, huh?"

"I'm in love with her," Cam replied with a hint of challenge in her voice.

Her mom's eyes briefly widened in surprise, before softening as if she knew how true that statement was. "I am happy for you. That's all we really want as parents—for our kids to be happy. If Riley does that for you, then that's great. I do like her, Cameron. I hope you know that my anger and fear was never about her. I know she is a good person. I've seen how good of a friend she has been to you and how well she treats your brothers. I haven't forgotten that throughout all of this.

"And ever since you've been dating Riley, I've noticed you've become more confident and you stand up for yourself more. I don't know if it's because of her or because you're just more comfortable with yourself, but I couldn't be prouder of you. You are turning into a remarkable young woman."

"Thanks, Mom. Hearing you say that means a lot to me. I think it's both. Riley is so good for me; we're good for each other, actually. But, I am so much more comfortable with myself. I'm not confused anymore. I know who I am."

Her mom smiled and nodded. "Well, I should let you get some sleep. You have a big day tomorrow."

Cam took a deep breath and let it out slowly. "Yeah, I do."

"Are you nervous?"

"About the ceremony? No, not really." Cam averted her gaze and looked at her hands in her lap.

"But, about what comes next?"

Cam let out a soft chuckle. "Maybe a little."

"That's totally normal. But, you're going to be great—in whatever you choose to do. Moving out and going to college will be a big change, but I will always be here for you. Whether you just need to come home for a break or you need a quick chat on the phone—never hesitate to let me know. Okay?"

"Okay."

She gently held Cam's face in her hands and Cam saw the admiration in her eyes right before her mom placed a soft kiss on her forehead. "Get some sleep, sweetie. I'll see you in the morning. Goodnight."

Her mom walked to the door, but she stopped at the doorway and pressed her hand against the frame as she turned at the sound of Cam's voice.

"I love you, Mom."

"I love you too."

* * *

They pulled into the school parking lot at the same time as Riley and her family. Riley's family walked toward the school entrance as Riley walked toward Cam, but she stopped immediately when she saw Cam's mom right behind her.

Her mom smiled at Riley and said, "It's okay."

That was the only thing Riley needed to hear before she quickly hugged Cam tightly.

"Everything okay?" she whispered in Cam's ear and she nodded.

As they broke apart, her mom walked over to them. "Riley, I would like to apologize to you. I know I've treated you unfairly and I've kept you from seeing Cam. I hope we can get to know each other a little better this summer before you head off to school."

"I'd like that, Ms. Leoni."

She wrapped Riley into a hug, and then held Riley by the shoulders, looking at her with a stony expression. "There still won't be any sleepovers. Got it?"

Riley straightened and said with a frightened look in her eyes, "Yes, ma'am."

Her mom gave her a wink and told them, "I'll see you two after the ceremony. Riley, tell your parents you're all welcome to join us for dinner tonight." Riley nodded, and Cam's mom walked away. "Oh, and make sure you two don't trip while you're on stage," she said with a chuckle.

"Thanks for the pep talk, Mom!" Cam called as she waved to the rest of her family.

Cam turned to Riley, grabbed her hands, and gave her a kiss. Riley looked into Cam's eyes and interlocked their fingers. "So, things with your mom have changed?"

Smiling broadly, Cam replied, "Yeah, we had a chat last night. I'll fill you in at dinner."

"Sounds great," she said, pulling Cam in for a lingering kiss. "Now, let's go graduate. Don't forget; don't trip!"

As Riley listened to speeches from the principal, valedictorian, and salutatorian, she couldn't keep a wide smile off her face. It wasn't because the speeches were great or she was excited to graduate and move on to the next phase of her life. It was because she knew something had changed in a major way between Cam and her mom. For the first time in months, when it came to her family, the smile that graced Cam's face fully reached her eyes.

While Riley knew Cam's mom had kept them apart whether she explicitly said so or not, Riley had never once held it against her. She knew from her own experience of coming out to her parents the fear and apprehension parents experienced when finding out their kid was queer. Her parents certainly didn't accept her sexuality right away, so she wasn't surprised that Ms. Leoni had struggled with everything as well. But, it meant the world to Riley to have Ms. Leoni apologize to her and give her a hug. To have one of the most important people in Cam's life show validation and approval for their relationship gave Riley a sense of happiness and peace.

Riley's mind returned to the present as the principal told the first row of students to stand and line up to receive their diplomas. Riley watched as the first fifteen students walked to the side of the stage at the bottom of the stairs. After the first five received their diplomas, a teacher at the end of Riley's row signaled the students to take their place in line. When Riley came to the bottom of the stairs, she took a deep breath as the advice not to trip echoed in her mind. She heard her name called and she stepped up to receive her diploma and shake the hand of the principal and vice principal.

As she made her way across the stage, she heard a high-pitched whistle come from the audience. She knew who it was immediately as her eyes searched her still-seated classmates. Finally, her gaze landed on a pair of big, beautiful brown eyes, and her breath caught in her throat when she saw the beaming smile that graced Cam's face. As she continued to stare, a matching smile formed, and she gave Cam a wink as she walked down the stairs at the other end of the stage. She took her seat again and released a deep breath. All she wanted to do at that moment was jump out of her chair again, so she could walk over and envelop Cam in a bone-crushing hug. But she felt that would be slightly frowned upon, so she sat back and waited impatiently for the ceremony to end.

To Cam's chagrin, the ceremony passed by slower than she would have liked. Once it ended, she made her way out of the gym to meet up with her family and friends, stopping every so often for a congratulatory hug from one of her classmates. She scanned the crowd on the way to a patch of grass which was the agreed upon meeting spot for her family.

She stopped when she saw her parents chatting with Riley's parents—and Claire and Riley talking animatedly together. If anyone had told her a few months ago, even just a few weeks ago, that this is the scene she would see after graduation, she would have thought they had lost their mind.

Before her thoughts had a chance to turn emotional, Claire yelled as she and Riley turned toward Cam with wide smiles. "Cameron Elizabeth, quit your dawdling! Let's get these pictures over with so we can go eat!"

Cam quickly walked to the group and received hugs and congratulations from everyone. As she finished with a quick kiss to Riley's cheek, her mother corralled everyone for pictures.

"Okay, girls. I want to get a few pictures of the three of you," her mom said as she held up her phone.

After about ten minutes of pictures in various groups and combinations, the parents all confirmed where they made reservations for dinner. Then everyone split up to go to their respective cars.

As Cam watched the families walk toward the parking lot, Riley reached for Cam's hand and faced her. "Everything okay?" she asked softly.

"I'm better than okay," she replied as she leaned in and kissed Riley tenderly.

"Good," Riley replied with that grin of hers. "Now, let's go. I'm starving and it's time to celebrate!"

It was hard to fathom how things had all come together as Cam was beginning to take the next step in her young adult life. Soon, she would be leaving the shelter of familiarity and embarking on a journey into the unknown. She was undoubtedly thankful to have the support of her family, Claire, and Riley.

While she knew the future could be unpredictable, she also knew that the beautiful girl holding her hand had been the bright light in a dark and difficult year. She knew that as long as she had Riley by her side, then everything else would fall into place. Being in different states for college would be a drastic change, but she knew they'd always be able to come back to each other. One look into Riley's eyes or a touch of her hand and Cam understood that would be all she needed to feel at home.

Bella Books, Inc.

Women. Books. Even Better Together.

P.O. Box 10543
Tallahassee, FL 32302

Phone: 800-729-4992
www.bellabooks.com